Nathalie Quintane
# **The Cavalier**

TRANSLATED FROM FRENCH BY JONATHAN LARSON

Winter Editions, 2025

# 1

It's so long ago. Another era. So unlike our own.

Why go back to a totally alien time when we so need something that speaks to us today?

That's what I said to myself, more than once, while I was assembling what you are about to read.

Most witnesses would agree, anyway, that it was another era, a closed case—you're dragging me back in time . . . That was more than forty years ago . . . Fifty years ago . . . I've never gone back to any of that . . .

\*

*No office job, and no teaching*: I begin by recopying the words I'd underlined almost two years ago now.

What would we call that, today? Principles? Limits? Ethics? A way of life by deduction or subtraction (if I eliminate *working an office job and teaching*, what's left)?

OK. The "no office job and no teaching," that didn't happen right away. Back then, it wasn't what came first and foremost; it was secondary. But to rediscover the first and foremost—which was vast, or of too considerable a scale to enter into our present parameters and be identified, recognized, as credible—one has to pass through what was secondary.

Since first and foremost was: *no work*.

It's a well-known phrase, tagged on a wall in 1968: Never work. It was a literary phrase; a tactical move to secure a minimum, the way one asks the boss for a six hundred euro raise to secure one hundred. A.k.a.: All right, fine, I'll work, if you insist, but not an office job and not in teaching.

And yet, the phrase, *no work*, was taken literally at the time, at face value.

The era: between 1969 and 1976, let's say (the year that Françoise (from Mézel) left for Dormillouse to live communally, without needing to work—Françoise, upon rereading, corrects: *to be employed*). There were other phrases, which said the same thing another way, for example:

> To live off nothing.
> DIY outside the system.
> It was getting by and the getting was good.
> To work is participation.

Dormillouse. A hamlet, in the Hautes-Alpes, near the Italian border, at 1700 meters. A hideout in other words. People went there first to hunt down Waldensians, in the fifteenth century, then Protestants. Four centuries of back-and-forth between periods of calm and massacres. For a long time, I asked myself how I, a teacher, could accurately describe to twelve-, thirteen-year-old seventh graders what happened there: how people used to kill each other where their parents would take them to see marmots and go mountain biking, both inside and right outside each other's homes. Back then, Catholics went around town in Gap with Protestant noses pinned to their hats, and ears, too: it's what I tell them, the seventh graders—the best I could come up with.

On Wikipedia, under Dormillouse, one finds traces of Françoise and her friends: [A community of young Protestants] was gradually supplanted in the early 1970s by hippies who often attracted the population's hostility. The last "bearded men" left Dormillouse in the late '70s (end of quote).

Sure, one might talk about the Waldensians in the same way one sums up the hippies. Well, the Waldensians must have had a rich life then, imagine that.

What talking about it with Philippe, Patrick, and others made clear was that, at least until 1973, the move to retreat was in no way made for lack of anything better or an acceptance of the failure of revolution and a negative tipping point—a retreat to smaller, more rural forms of life; something more manageable, in essence. No. It was in anticipation of the revolution, which would be coming soon (Philippe: Every evening we'd tell ourselves: tomorrow morning it's due).

The revolution never came, or, as Françoise says: it didn't happen; still, the feeling that things can be changed remained.

If May '68 (March 1871, June 1848, July 1830, '89, etc.) was something people did, then it's possible, and if it was possible, it's something we can do again.

Even so, it's striking, the kind of aquarium all of us were living in from 1983 to 1995, with our sails unfurled between plastic rocks and air pumps.

The question I kept asking myself, while they were talking, was: How did they do it, to live off nothing? What does it mean concretely, to live off nothing? Béa explains their initial rent of 150 francs; the public showers; they salvaged; there were gypsies whose sheds stood next to the public dump (that, I knew about in the mid-'90s; eventually solid buildings were put up for them, always next to the dump (now the waste management center), like in *The Castafiore Emerald* in the Adventures of Tintin) . . . The gypsies used to do the sorting: on one side they sold; and on the other you picked through the trash heap. No one repaired anything. Everything was salvaged. Béa remembers a point in time when she sold cakes, at the market. Jewelry perhaps, with pearls.

Françoise: We used to sell chestnuts on the way to the train station; we stole food; whenever you got hungry, you went to the market, whatever they tossed out. The day she arrived in town by chance (she was supposed to meet a friend there), she asked around at the bar: You wouldn't know where I could stay the night, would you? They lived as a group, smoked weed, the cops tried hard to catch them, never did though. This is how they lived in the city between ages eighteen and twenty-two, without feeling poor.

Several years ago, I went and saw a photography exhibition, don't ask me where, I no longer remember, but there I happened on a series of old negative prints, from the early twentieth century, taken in South America, most likely in Tierra del Fuego: first, the compatriots from distant lands, around a fire clad in hides and in high spirits; then, several months later, these same ones, dressed in European fashion and looking down-and-out.

Perhaps, as I listened to them, I first noted down what I found unsurprising, what I had anticipated corroborating, what I had come to corroborate, the flat refusal of the years 1969–1973 for example, followed by the long descent, a withering aimlessness which, in the long run, pressures you into negotiating, not to disown yourself (no one, in this group, did, save for perhaps the writer— although he may say that he had in no way disowned the first part of his existence as a writer since, after all, he still continued to write, just not the same books, books that are more accessible but where a kind of continuity is dimly perceptible (in the bitterness, right? I would have clarified had I met him), and wasn't that, all said and done, a logical outcome, once the temptation of suicide had been ruled out, or somehow or other brought to an end—what do you think? Not cynically: at a distance. Writing for people in general, people you run into every day at your bakery or your insurance company, and not a coterie that lives between the fifth and sixth arrondissement (he presumably wouldn't put it that way, but that's the gist).

I see, highlighted in neon yellow, phrases I remember not surprising me: when Béa says they all used to share a collective spirit; they lived, somewhat, in community . . . Together, in D., renting a shared studio where everyone did painting, weaving, and so on, but the same people always paid, and eventually the floor caved in. Only afterward (or at the same time?) did she have to live with Lélen, separated from Cathy, in the shed, no water and no electricity, with kerosene lamps, those years that Garrel was filming Nico\* in dark houses, by the fire, striking up her little harmonium.

When I went up to see Béa, the structure had extended up and out around the shed; cubes and volumes open on all sides, east, west, south, north, so the sun comes in at every hour of the day, whenever there's daylight. From the patio, you can fly out over the valley, gazing out across a paradise. At your back, there's the garden shed, its window open a crack onto the room where Patrick and Lélen listened to Coltrane on a portable radio set, jamming together, tapping out the rhythms on plates, and then there was the day Patrick brought his guitar: Oh no! He's going to play us pieces he

---

\* Phillippe Garrel: *La Cicatrice intérieure* (*The Inner Scar;* 1972), *Les Hautes Solitudes* (*The High Solitudes;* 1974). Nico : *Desertshore* (1971), *The End* (1974).

learned! Jazz, because life is improvised: there's no score. Moving on, here are the reclaimed windows Béa pieced together, the doorjambs' flaky paint, the round or oval handles, the square and rectangular panes; they raised see-through walls made from a great mass of bric-à-brac where they have—where they had tea. Young Lélen used to draft houses for friends, dove headfirst into every project—a harpsichord factory—with gusto. Refused to complete his architecture degree. He did end up becoming a teacher at the art school, but only so he could drag his students outside, to go salvaging, and to discuss, to analyze. Stephen, who had him as a teacher for ten years: school, it's just someplace you drop your bag. More a locker than a barracks.

His colleagues used to say he was "opposed to practicing the trade," but his house was a work in itself (or what they call an art piece), and Patrick adds that 70 percent of his house was him, that without seeing it no one would be able to understand what it meant for him to live.


Béa, sitting across from me at the kitchen table:
—I can't really say what we lived off, to tell the truth.


Perhaps that's just it, "living off nothing": saying, forty years later, when all is said and done, no one really knows what any of us lived off. No one knows, because no one remembers, and no one remembers because no one saw it as important—less important than you or me, anyway, we who save or spend without keeping track or just survive, but always with this money consciousness, this superimposed image of money, sublime value.

Be that as it may, in the early 1990s, a friend of theirs, a student of Lélen's, pitched his tent, not far from the shed, winter to summer, for two years. Well, the rent was free and he didn't feel like working, is how Béa puts it. At the core was just that: it's free, and you don't feel like working yourself to the bone—the core.

Did they all use to be this disinterested? Patrick had mentioned one guy who was less disinterested—but it's only the disinterested who interest me—co-founder of L'Occitane who had made a fortune, boutiques in every airport reaching all the way to the U.S., to China. A straightforward entrepreneurial career path, whose wide swerves two booksellers will bring to light in April 2021: he shipped soap molds, courtesy of a bankrupt company, to Paris for free, that's how he started out, in the mid-'70s; as soon as that started picking up and the operation industrialized, he would sell, buy, and start over again; at his first factory he hired fringe characters from around the way, addicts, "misfits." His own nonconformist parents had moved there to go off the grid, long before Cathy, Béa, or Françoise arrived in the area.

I never got the impression, from their comments, that he belonged to any groups—not the group of brains or the group of junkies, of course. Perhaps he was willingly deceptive when opportunity presented itself: the opportunity for a coffee at Le Grand Café or a discussion on the boulevard, all while thinking about how to get himself out of there and the sooner the better.

To get oneself out of there and the sooner the better: catchphrase of the young, ages twenty-one to twenty-eight, here—and yes, at twenty-eight if you still haven't left, it's over. But it wasn't like that back then, says Françoise from Mézel, people used to come up from Aix or from Marseille, they would debate in the cafés, even if, like anywhere else, it was always the same ones that spoke up, at pains to place the right words in the right places, all the words that needed placing, says Françoise, who is still the fieriest one to this day, passionate about Rudolf Steiner's pedagogy, who recounts both an exciting and miserable childhood with brio (it was just awful). It is she who turns up, I recall, asking: You wouldn't know where I could stay the night, would you? A time she's unlikely to forget, because that's where she runs into Robert, little Robert (not that old . . . eighteen or nineteen). Robert and Michel X., an important guy in the affair (he was the brother of the other guy, Thierry). She describes them as "the leftmost left"; the implication is still the same today as it was back then: anarchists. They used to spend around two weeks preparing for May Day, and this was no doubt the only time the black flag flew over the boulevard. Purgatory for anarchy, as a coherent body of thought and a way of life, will last another good thirty years—or century, even.

The X.'s: two brothers. One of them was pointed out

to Nelly since she was on the lookout for a builder, or rather, for a handyman to do the building, right after she bought the space in the town center. Two friends, who were in their thirties, had just bought a building in the middle of the night, in the middle of nowhere, with a dormitory. A dormitory. Less a dream of community than of just in case. For settling down or shirking work. Fixer-uppers are fairly affordable in France, but friends in their thirties, shy, insecure, threatened, prefer living in the countryside, far away. Béa and Nelly though set up in town—they weren't the problem, nor was the way of life they were promoting; that one could live like this, and live well at that: proof. The two units they purchased, though unmanaged, were ultimately their tools of propaganda.

Michel, in the early 1970s, was a schoolteacher with a herd of goats. Not for show: his family were farmers. The X.'s were the proles of the gang. To have a herd of goats as a schoolteacher wasn't out of the norm, but it was that he—being cultivated, and a queer just like his brother—went and became a schoolteacher in the first place. Françoise unintentionally joined the circle of "drug addicts," who were always smoking and whom the cops used to try and catch—if I set drug addicts in quotation marks, it's because it's the ignominious mark that identified them, by which in turn I guess they were identified, and which permitted them to position themselves against the second group, the "brains" (the brains were supposedly able to smoke without becoming perma-fried). Françoise describes the line that separated the two groups as a hard limit: two ways of relating to the world with a contempt that cut both ways. But Vincent tells me he was able to move back-and-forth between the groups. Françoise writes, at the end of the first version of this text: the border between the two groups existed implicitly, hazily, and was constantly shifting, to be crossed only with great difficulty. She rounds out the group: it was "hippies, dropouts, anarchists" . . . who either worked odd jobs (artisans, precarious side gigs . . .) or did not ("low-lifes"), who would come together around reefer or weed, shutting themselves in for the day at their downtown pads, rock music turned all the way up. They were in revolt against the entire system. The drug of choice: only weed, none of the hard drugs of the '80s, she specifies.

Sure enough, the following decade saw carnage descend upon the Sud-Est.


I put myself in the skin of the second group: the brains would eventually prevail, with capitalism again triumphant in the world, not only because they had degrees, or adequate intellectual defenses, but also because they sought to understand the world as it is, which is already a form of participation. The drug addicts now, five years on, maintained Blanchot's position in '68, that of a radical refusal, of a comma-less No.* So I put myself in the skin of the first group: maybe they saw a kind of capitulation in the second group.

But intellectual resistance used to be as much a part of general resistance as anything else, they nurtured and trained each other. The only way to hold out in what was to come, from 1973 onwards, as in a foggy period, a latent period, of subdued opposition, was to connect the two and let go of neither—precisely what the Germans, and then the Swiss finally did, on their side of the hill, only an hour's drive away.

Françoise (from Mézel) didn't last long out there, with the Swiss, after the fall from grace (her choice of words) in the backwaters, even though they were all between eighteen and twenty-two years old at the time (and should be considered minors, even after 1974 came and went, given the time it takes for laws or social transformations to be assimilated, their approval notwithstanding—as it was, the hassle of getting an abortion lasted well after the Veil law legalized it). The closest commune, geographically speaking, used to be the Swiss one, and it was only natural to go have a look around once the feeling of shuffling in place had started to take hold in

---

* Jean-François Hamel, *Nous sommes tous la pègre. Les années 68 de Blanchot* [We Are All Rabble: Blanchot's '68 Years] (Minuit, 2018). "At some point, in the face of public events, we know we must refuse. The refusal is absolute, categorical. It does not argue, nor does it present its reasons" (Maurice Blanchot).

the mid-'70s. The community we're talking about, then, wasn't of the flower power variety: close-combat, revolutionary chants in German, and if you didn't know what you wanted to do, you split—their leader, he himself had dealt with *real* Nazis: one must always be prepared for their return; and that was both his lesson, and the community's. What amazed and amused us only five years ago, struck me as true wisdom, as something we'd do well to acknowledge. Physical and intellectual training was their original program, to which, depending on the moment, they remained more or less faithful, whenever the flocks and fields left them enough time to read and pick fights.

I hated phys ed, I didn't know how to run, and while maneuvering the ropes, I always wound up upside-down. I liked to swim, of course, but that's useless when a battalion of riot cops are at your heels. CRS agents do 100-meter sprints at people, during protests. It's strange, like a herd of elephants charging onto a deserted parking lot and kicking up dust (or in this case tear gas). Stéphane no longer wants me to go to protests in Paris: It's too dangerous. On top of that I wear contact lenses, I'm myopic. In May 2019 (that said, Leslie proffers, May Day is a family affair!), I wanted to see for myself: Would I keep up? Would I panic? I took my swimming goggles and a scarf. Just making our way into the protest was a challenge; we could see the union confederation CGT's big balloon from a distance, but a cordon of police officers blocked the entrance onto the boulevard. After some time, we got through. We marched, passing by small groups of various allegiances and raising chants that lifted you off the ground at heart level. At one point, we got stopped up like we were waiting in a cafeteria line. The crowd grew behind us and there was no movement forward—after twenty-five years of cafeterias, that's something I've become accustomed to. All of a sudden, I saw flying saucers, small ones, launched over the crowd—canisters of tear gas. Everyone did a one-eighty, we were all driven back. There, we found ourselves thronged from the front, thronged from behind, budging not one bit. I said to myself: Patience, there's nothing you can do now anyway. Our feet that we couldn't see shuffled ahead, inch by inch. I put on my goggles and clutched my scarf tight. I breathed as little as possible, like when you're crossing somewhere foul-smelling—a stinky street, factory, beet fields in the north. After several meters, a big white gate, outside hôpital Salpêtrière. I said to myself: It's over, we're all going to be crushed against the fence. I had to think of Heysel.* And then two young guys quickly climbed over the iron gate, shook it, got the lock to break, and it was open.

We presumably used to run for no other reason than to finish first, at school, then to keep in shape, after office hours, and now, for the first time, to flee from blows, the beatdowns delivered by these indistinct columns dressed in black and blue, police become cops, cops

---

* On May 29 1985, at Heysel stadium (Brussels), during the European Cup Final, the separating fence and a low wall collapsed under the fans' weight and pressure, resulting in 39 deaths and 400 injuries.

become vigilantes, republican or fascist, do they know, who knows?

Françoise, meanwhile, did not see herself running marathons through the woods, jumping over tree stumps, aiming at targets, training dogs: in 1976, she and Robert cleared out to the Ardèche after a two-month camp partially funded by Robert, who worked construction and odd jobs for about a year. The Ardèche lasted two years in total, until September 1978; there they received training as cobblers in Romans (the city of shoes) and then Robert finally opened a shoe repair in the sticks, for seven or eight years (this would be the mid-'80s). It must have been toward the end of the summer or the beginning of fall 1977 that they found themselves mixed up in something with which they had nothing to do but which somehow had everything to do with them: the story of Pierre Conty.

Forty years later I'm watching the news of August 26, 1977, delivered by Jean-Claude Bourret. I was thirty at the time; the mood of the nightly news remains all too familiar. They're looking for Conty; he keeps slipping through their fingers. Bourret turns up the heat: Conty, *the Ardèche killer*. Conty, the Ardèche killer; immediately it rings a bell—but why? Bourret recaps: Conty = neo-rural = hippie = marginal = thief = (potential) killer = no surprises => someone to fear => but fear not => instead, assist the police.

He's described as a "gypsy type," and I found him to bear a striking resemblance to Pierre Clémenti, only rougher around the edges. Conty was a prole from Grenoble, from a family of communist workers. After 1968, he left (there were a thousand and one departures, all of them singular; Christiane Rochefort imagines one in her novel, *Springtime in the Parking Lot*, which I'll come back to). He settled in the Ardèche with some buddies (judging by the photos, they were not many), raised goats on land no one cared for, got involved with farmers in the area, and along with two "community members" he committed a holdup in the Lozère, at a Crédit Agricole branch, which ended badly: three dead, including a policeman. He was never caught, but at the end of his Wikipedia entry, I read: "Christian Bonnet, Minister of the Interior in 1977, enigmatically declared about him at a press conference: 'He will do no more harm,'" suggesting that he had been taken down by former comrades or by the French intelligence services.

Back home after travels in Spain, Robert and Françoise happen on some cops as they were literally trashing their place: she allegedly slipped some cash to Conty, seen at the neighborhood post office. A completely unrelated letter (from a local friend, someone who appears a little earlier in this text) is interpreted as a confirmation. The investigation goes nowhere. I noted, and underlined, that Conty had tried to create something politicized—holding firmly to the principle that the land belongs to whomever cultivates it, for example. I can't keep myself from thinking that the Germans (Swiss) were cleverer:

they purchased the land themselves at the outset. No one could come and claim it from them.

In commemoration of fifty years of May '68, a radio broadcast revisits the "crazy Ardèche killers" affair. At the branch, nothing is off, they get the money, but according to the black and white magic of the unconscious, the three are backed into a corner with or by a police van and Conty takes down the driving officer. He doesn't just stop there though, he proceeds to drag a father and his son out of their car and takes them down, too, them and no one else, at least not that anyone has seen. The radio explains it was fine people at the time such as Jean-Paul Sartre who were justifying the use of political violence—a revolution has never been made without violence—that the evidence was not only pointing to the coming revolution, but first it pointed to civil war in France, on the horizon of 1970–1972. The radio rambles and chuckles and laughs at the lagging behind of these young characters, hell-bent on nurturing a defunct effervescence in a world that has since returned to routine. Today, i.e., two years after the broadcast, now the program lags behind: political violence is bursting out everywhere; a civil war in France is no less possible than an insurrection—one year I remember in particular, Christmas 2018, when I had used the words "uprising" and "insurrection" on the subject of the Yellow Vests around my family and had been laughed at. Six months later, my family was quoting these same words back to me.

# 2

The affair (which is why I am writing all this now and evidently in the utmost chronological disorder) has been known to me for a long time, a long time ago Patrick told me about it, briefly, at least whatever had made its way to him, since he was no longer in the sticks by then—in 1975–1976, he was away at college. Needless to say, I haven't the faintest recollection of what one thing led to another, that led him to tell me about it one day while standing on the boulevard, most likely after the farmer's market, on a Wednesday or Saturday. Was this book on the Éducation nationale, the French educational system, already on my mind? Did he immediately associate this project with the event, one of the few events that marked the town's judicial chronicle, apart from the Dominici affair?\* Knowing me as a poet, with an interest in news oddities and documents, did he see a supplementary text, a logical work, in line with what I'd already written, and which was interesting to him, because it's precisely situated, historically, geographically (right here at home, even) and is revealing—of what? That's the whole point

---

\* The "Dominici affair," named after Gaston Dominici, a peasant accused of triple homicide in the vicinity of his farm in the commune of Lurs in 1952.

of literature, to reveal only what can be revealed by inching along and without thinking of the process as a "revelation" anyway, but rather as the excavation of things one happens on because they happen on you. In short, was it an order?

Maybe it was history's immediate seduction, the immediate seduction of its name, that held me back—it was too much, it felt like fiction, and I didn't work in fiction. Patrick brought it up numerous times. He tried baiting me: this young woman, pretty, leftist, highly qualified agrégée teacher, in a long black cape, I was bound to bite—all these years, every time it came to mind, I saw the long black cape, out in the sticks, because it was (is) a hurdle we all had to overcome, and because of Zorro (righter of wrongs who emerges from the night, toward adventure). All these years, I said to him maybe, no, I said to myself maybe and then no. What right of mine was it to go digging around in a town's past, a town that hates nothing more than someone digging around, even if I did run into and hear firsthand from those who had at one point entered that history which Nelly herself had, in a way, entered, to leave them with a black and white memory?


One day, in 2014 or 2015, in a junk shop at Saint-Étienne, I see Stephen move toward me with a book hoisted like a trophy: *Élements pour une analyse du fascisme/2, séminaire de Marie-A. Macciocchi Paris VII - Vincennes 1974–1975*, from Éditions 10/18. I say to him: Yea, great,

thank you!
 —No, this isn't it! Look what's inside!
 On the flyleaf, in ink, some fifteen handwritten lines:

> D. A teacher of Φ at the lycée of D., Mme Nelly Cavallero, was charged with the "incitement of minors to debauchery" by an investigating judge of the municipal court.
>
> Mme Cavallero would lend her place of residence to a known homosexual who received young people there. The latter, X., charged with "indecent assault of a minor under fifteen years of age," was the subject of an arrest warrant. [*Midi Libre*, Wednesday, March 23, 1976].

Right. So I would have to re-become a surrealist then?
 As for this coincidence, or objective chance, I don't put much stock in it. I would always come back to: maybe—and then, no.
 But in April 2017, while I was participating in a literature festival in Grenoble and waiting for potential customers at a stand, I saw a lady approaching, in her sixties, vivacious, who, at some point in the conversation, said something like: When I hear D., my mind goes straight to the Cavallero affair!
 The fact that she still remembered this case forty years later wasn't just because I'm from D., a three-hour drive from Grenoble, whichever way one skirts the Col de Lus, and it wasn't just because I'm a teacher, because

Nelly used to be a teacher, and Françoise, the lady from Grenoble, used to be a teacher: it was because she, Françoise, had her license pulled by the Éducation nationale five years before Nelly, in 1971. What stayed with me: one woman lost her license . . . two women lost their licenses . . . How many had lost their licenses in total, specifically between 1969 and 1976?

From experience, and like something parroted without understanding, I said to myself, ever since entering the institution in '86: you could do anything, short of beating up an entire class, and still not get fired from the Éducation nationale and even then, word would have to get out. And since I was giving lessons in the customary places (in towns, in countrysides), whose fragile equilibrium depends essentially on the fact that word never gets out (about anything of importance, that is), it could be inferred that no one but a strange woman whose life was entirely devoted to the search for and public expression of the truth could have had her teaching license revoked, especially between 1969 and 1976.

I was taken aback, three years ago, by the anguished look on my mother's face when she learned I was going to Nuits debout*:

—You, a teacher, in a small town, have to keep a low profile: you could lose your job.

The anxiousness welled up in her not from the depths

---

* Nuit debout: movement of the squares (assemblies, occupations, demonstrations) without a spokesperson or leader, which took place in France between March and June 2016.

of time but directly from the 1950s; from the post-war years, in a town only slightly larger than the one I live in (and where Nelly lived, from September 1974 to June 1976): the neighbor's curtains raised a touch for passing girls; the scandal and the indelible shame that arise when a mistake is made, sexual mistakes most of all which redound to the family; the preoccupation with debauchery among Caths and Communists alike; abortion and contraception bans promoted by both; guys got a beating and girls got curls; the peril one risks by engaging in politics, in unionizing; it doesn't go over well; one risks one's job; unemployment is poverty—and poverty, yes, thank you, we know what that is: meticulously picking at bones once the kids have eaten the meat; traveling six kilometers every morning to bring home milk; the precious egg the chicken lays. The story goes that an ordinance ended the Vichy regime in August of 1944, and that at any rate the Republic never ceased existing in law. That's not how I feel about it. I've neither felt nor understood (here it amounts to the same thing) how what made the regime what it was came to an end abruptly the same way it came into existence, by decree. The experienced bounds do not coincide with the bounds of the law. When one prefers not to "engage in politics," not to unionize, for fear of losing one's job or being "hassled," one no longer lives in a democracy—that's all that counts. Which doesn't mean much because then belonging to a union or engaging in politics is to live in a democracy. So long as someone has good reason to fear the public expression of certain ideas (ideas as simple as: there are poor people; I know where the money is), we will not be in a democracy—or a "democracy" like the one Rimbaud puts in quotation marks in 1872, to the sound of drums, trumpets, and colonial terror. To nuance the point: for fifty years, from 1968 to 2018, my family may have been wrong to think it would be better *not to*. Nowadays, I can only concede: saying certain things publicly will cost you an eye, a hand, a job. The bizarre arbitrariness of bureaucracy will remove you from what you live on, from where you live (you can no longer afford the cost, so you live in your car; but you are kept from living in your car, so you move to the street; but you are kept from living in the street, etc.). And the markets will recoup whatever is left.

And yet things aren't so cut-and-dried. That between 1968 and 2018 (or 2016) it was altogether wrong (we can spare ourselves the details) to think one was living anywhere else than in a democracy is thwarted by the Cavallero affair and its context.

This text could have been written out of thwartedness. A situated, historical thwartedness, at a weak moment of History (the institutions are afraid and when they are afraid, they lash out). It's as if, right after May, two diametrically opposed convictions, positioned back-to-back, had jumped into the place feet first: on the one side, the May folks, persuaded that—the civil war and the revolution being for tomorrow—they had to go all the way; on the other, the harnessed counter-insurrection of neoliberalism, convinced it was the moment to restore order and go all in, without holding back, by any means, etc.

What surprised me, once I had grown truly interested in the ins and outs of Françoise's (from Grenoble) and Nelly's backstories, a little more than a year ago, in fall 2018, was the carefree way they went about things, holding flowers up to guns, whoopsie daisy, having barely set foot in the institution and they're already making their move, coolly gunning for it—abortion, contraception, open discussions with students, and not just at any high schools, either, even at the uptight schools stuck in the 1950s and one not founded yet: a reputable lycée in Grenoble; a typically puritanical lycée in D.

I see Bernadette Lafont, in one such '70s flick, her smile like sucking candy, crossing the Stendhal Museum courtyard in a miniskirt and boots; or there was Bulle, Bulle Ogier, in the famous very last sequence of *The Salamander*\* (final sequence before the revolution, 1971), when the owners of the shoe store she worked at whisper to her (we want no scenes here): You're not working in this store a minute longer . . . Are you crazy . . . You little bitch . . . and then she responds loudly in a childish voice: **Oui, Monsieur! Oui, Madame! Oui, Monsieur! I can't believe it** (whispers the lady) **Goodbye Mademoiselle, goodbye Monsieur, merci beaucoup beaucoup!** Bulle's smiles, in the crowd, which are directed at no one but herself, at the skilled hand

---

\* Alain Tanner, *La Salamandre*, 1971. Final sequence: <https://www.youtube.com/watch?v=zL3BqggqfXs>.

she played, at her competent sass. And the text in voice *off*: *Today was December 20. The holidays, as they are called, were looming on the horizon. The commodity was forcing its laws on the crowd, which was fighting its way into the stores. It was the time of year when a marked tendency toward schizophrenia was most pronounced, a phenomenon that tended more and more to afflict the social body as a whole. There was no snow yet, which was basically normal for that time of year.*

Too bad you have no guitar—this is what Patrick would have said: Nath, you can retranscribe all you want, but with no guitar, they won't understand, because it's the guitar, the electric guitar, that brings out the desire in that sequence, and the desire, in 1971, is to destroy everything, the rage that everything should instantly become as it had been before, and the desire to maintain over and against everything.

In 1991, a film by Philippe Garrel: *I don't hear the guitar anymore.*

I go back to the "I can't believe it" of the store owner. I read an explanation for it yesterday evening when I began Grégoire Chamayou's book *The Ungovernable Society*. There he talks about the Lordstown wildcat strikes, in the U.S., when the bosses decided to put the screws to the workers, who were young and a little too loose, in the early 1970s: one of them is suspended for farting inside of a car; another for yodeling on the shop floor. But in March 1972, the guys *became tigers*: they had no fear of management. That's the difference: for several years, and up until at least 1973, young people, workers, employees, teachers . . . were no longer afraid. Facing them, and for the first time in their lives, the little bosses, higher ups, owners, principal and vice-principal, the inspectors and respectable family fathers encountered the sovereign gaze of those who were done being afraid.

## 3

There she is, Nelly, walking up the boulevard in a way that says *It's my ass and I do what I want* amid sullen glares, smirks, idle gazes, bell bottoms on early day stoners. Vincent told me that once, at a local Rencontres Cinéma screening, upon viewing the nice dick of an actor on-screen who of course also happened to be in the theater, she said to him (loudly, to be sure): Damn, that dick of his is nice, I need it! Duly noted.

Patrick enjoys dishing the sordid details of the era—these were more political than the moral turpitude of the village Stals\* who griped about the leftists—that time the hitchhiker girl was headed to Draguignan, and going out of her mind with boredom, but then managed to touch herself until she came with nothing but the seam of her jeans (this Patrick told me loud and clear in a full restaurant, in D.). She was a tough one, anyway, and her jeans must have been really tight.

It's possible that without that first article in the *Nice-Matin*, popularly known as Nice-Putain, or Nice-Whore,

---

\* Diminutive of "Stalinist" (pejorative used to designate those who were still members of the French Communist Party).

the Cavallero affair would not have been nor would this text, which I am now writing and you are now reading. The article in question was not in the file (a faded orange folder with elastic bands) that Vincent lent me, and which serves as my true point of departure: combing through the era's press coverage—a half-dozen clippings, columns and full pages, snippets and shocking headlines dated March 1976. I hand them over to you without the spectacular bodies, for this work is not the revival of a scandal nor even that of a news oddity but a current update for the here and now.

> The "philosophy teacher" of D. is charged . . . with incitement of minors to debauchery (*Ici Paris*).
> The depraved archangel loses the title "philosophy teacher" (*France Soir*).
> Tempers run high in D. after the arrest of a lycée "prof" for inciting minors to debauchery (*unknown title*).
> Demon with an angel's face / One of her young victim's confessions: "I was fifteen, she introduced me to things I didn't know about" / Picked up at an entrance gate by Nelly, the philosophy teacher (*France Dimanche*).
> D. in the Grips of Depravity / The Black Sheep and La Pasionaria (*Le Monde*, March 7–8, 1976).
> Three columns in *Hara-Kiri*: Liberalism in Reverse / A Rag Acts Out (allusion to *Nice-Matin*).

> "D.—Two Hands" . . . Three charges (including Nelly Cavallero's) of public indecency (*unknown title*).

Online, I would happen upon a later *Le Monde* issue (November 5, 1976), in which the journalist summarizes: "Incitement of Minors to Debauchery," March 2, 1976. "Affront to Public Decency in the Press," March 10, 1976. "Indecent Exposure," July 1976, and an extract copied out, ironically, from *Ici Paris*: "The orgies tended to be frequent and marijuana cigarettes would pass often from mouth to couch and back through the night, a tangle of bodies exhaling love . . ."

What Vincent told me, the next time we saw each other, several months later, was that, on the one hand, the tabloids had attracted the eyes of the Parisian journalists and that, on the other, "no one had sized up the impact [Nelly's] network would have."

Paris was not of this world, but Nelly, she was certainly from Paris.

It's Vincent who receives the journalist from the *Nouvel Obs* at Le Grand Caf' and recounts what happened:

—So nothing happened then, there's no story! the guy says to him, and gives up.

There was nothing to the story, Vincent concludes. For a guy from Paris, this woman and what happened to her were nothing. And this momentous encounter, this radical opening and radical rupture in his life that was to accompany him until the end, until he hands me this old faded orange file folder, containing newspaper clippings and his Vaché/Rigaut/Cravan 10/18 pocketbook edition,* Nelly's gift to the young man of twenty he was back then. For a Parisian, it's nothing. He told me about the writer's arrival, who had briefly been a French high school teacher, down from Paris, and his remark: I pull into D. and there's only one boulevard! (I correct: there's not *only one*, there's two). The writer is thought to have more or less gotten himself fired by the Education ministry, in the early 1970s—it's true: I was able to find his name again on the (long) list of the expelled and suspended which the educational review *L'École émancipée* put out as a book with Maspero in 1972, *Repression in Education*.

*Val-d'Oise*: Y., a certified teacher of modern letters at the lycée of Gonesse, has just been suspended, with pay, by ministerial ruling, for professional misconduct. He was reprimanded for allowing things in his class to get too out of hand, for not following the curriculum, for letting students that were not his into his classes, for not notifying the school principal of his absences (*Le Monde*, February 9, 1972).

---

* *Trois suicidés de la société/Arthur Cravan, Jacques Rigaut, Jacques Vaché* [Three suicides of society] (Éditions 10/18, 1974).

Vincent restores the atmosphere: You'd go to school and after, to this café, where the middle-class locals went . . . You'd mingle with the teachers there . . . We'd have lunch at the philosophy teacher's, a young guy from Avignon. That was in the air, and it boosted our confidence . . . That was the norm.

I ask him how many teachers, in his view, tried to teach "otherwise" (the proportion is my obsession): four or five, not even . . . But, he adds, there were teachers who would be more discreet about it . . . who would go about it more discreetly.

I don't think there's been any change in proportion: four or five out of sixty or seventy is what I've been accustomed to my whole life and can attest to from my career. I remember my friend Anne, getting worked up over just how reactionary and irredeemably right-wing her son's teachers were now, they give him two-hundred, three-hundred lines to copy out in 2015, and not for detention! But why should teachers be any different from the rest of the population? The only distinctive thing about them is that they went through enough schooling to become teachers, but not enough to become more than teachers: they're yesterday's good students. I was one. I felt at ease in the school system just the way it was, and if I didn't, I wouldn't have stayed here so long. To understand how a child or an adolescent might feel unwell or suffer at school, from school, I have to make an effort: I have to put myself in their place. Hélène, who encountered Nelly at the time of the affair, was a long-time nursery school teacher at the start of her career;

adhered to the Freinet method*: No way I'm going to do what they did to me, she says, brushing aside the sadness of her school years.

—Nelly, for us, was Paris, Vincent continues.

To understand this phrase, I also have to make an effort. As a suburbanite, Paris was next door to me, both the same climate and same instantaneousness of urbanization and also altogether different journeys; both nearby and another world.

Vincent helps me out: We were mesmerized by Paris . . . It represented freedom . . . someplace else . . . It was a goal.

Back then, Paris was ten hours away by train.

One day, Nelly said something to him that may have been meant as a mere formality, something perfunctory: We'll have to go up to Paris together sometime.

Now Paris is less far away; but just a little less far. A two-hour drive to the TGV, which takes three hours from Aix-en-Provence. The tickets aren't cheap. When the young woman from whom I buy dried sausages at the market spoke to me about her weekend in Paris, she told me she visited the Louvre on the same day the Gilets jaunes protesters were there. Otherwise she prefers Corsica.

---

* Freinet pedagogy: a series of techniques developed by Célestin Freinet from the 1920s on, founded on children's free expression. Some of these techniques were taken up again bit by bit in high schools and middle schools (school papers, group work, abolishing the podium . . .). The school of Freinet is collaborative and emancipatory. Cf. n. 33 of the review *De(s)générations/Pédagogies émancipatrices* [(De)Generations/Emancipatory Pedagogies], Saint-Étienne, 2020.

I often recount the scene Lélen and I experienced together more than fifteen years ago, when I had been living in town for some time already: at an opening, plenty of people, everyone's greeting each other, he pauses for a moment, then unleashes: You, here? What do you think you're doing here, in D.? Why are you here? Thrown off, I stammer out some explanation: Well, I got transferred! There was a position that had just opened up at the high school . . . I had the points . . . He leaves me there, disturbed by the brunt of his interpellation. It took me some time to piece together the subtext—the implications. Nelly's history, her relation to the town, gave me one more key. It wasn't the fact that I was a teacher that bugged Lélen: of teachers who come along, there are plenty. No, it was that by then (actually, just as I arrived in D.) I'd started writing, not novels—let alone regional novels, like the writer. I'd ultimately started writing weird stuff like what you're now reading, which a Parisian publisher, P.O.L., published and in looking at any of my bios one can easily fact-check that I was born there, in Paris. So I was necessarily Parisian. Anywhere else than Paris, one must justify being from there, which is normal. It's normal only because it's fair—at some point living in Paris leads to a colonial relationship with the provinces.

So, childhood and adolescence in the suburbs (Department 93: Seine-Saint-Denis, once a red suburb, now a "no-go zone" for the nationalist right; and next 95: Val-d'Oise, a lower and middle class department with two regional parks and one-fourth of Roissy CDG airport). Relation of a commuter to Paris, which is to say a provincial relation. Leaving the banlieue at twenty-two in order to be a teacher, first up in the north, in Dunkirk, and in the provinces from there forward. Regular visits to the capital to go to museums, the cinema, and later to author gigs. I've never had a Paris address. Had Lélen seen Nelly through me? Was it that nearly forty years after the incidents, he regretted having supported and contributed to the drafting and distribution of the incendiary tract *D. Deux mains*? Did he regret having contributed to and deepening, via the tract, the town's humiliation?

The next time I see her, Béa tells me that's not the case at all, that I'm mistaken. Lélen would never have asked "what do you think you're doing" but "what brings you." And he was always excited to see other people in D. He was excited, but also surprised (that I stayed).

It's true, normally I wouldn't have stayed. I should have left—D., it doesn't take long to have seen the whole town—but leave, for where? It's what I always asked myself, and each time I told myself I wouldn't be staying, anyway, staying in the same place for that long, it doesn't make sense, there are other places to go—but go where? I would always blunder against the where. I couldn't find anywhere else. I was well aware of the kind of deserts that cities are, there's Paris, there's Lisbon—and there's D. One does the same things there, in the same order, in expanded or reduced fashion; so what?

My days of world exploration possibly came to an end with my first trip outside Europe: an off-season ticket, an empty four-star hotel waiting to be refilled, on Saint-Martin, in the French Antilles. Several days for going back and forth from room to beach, and then a question arises: what else is there, beyond the hotel, its palm trees, its lawns, its closed-off grounds? Where's the city? Where's the island? Where am I? So I rent a car, an automatic, and I set off for the island. Rutted roads, their potholes, un-tarmacked, a slum, on the left, four metal sheets and a Black man smoking in the entryway, in tattered clothes, off in the distance the city, its main street... nothing but jewelry stores. Jewelry stores to the right, jewelry stores to the left, and beaten earth in the middle. Was this some kind of *joke*? I should have said to myself something like: OK. Got it. So this is it?

In D., now, the jumbled mess of the commercial zone, with its GDR-style warehouses; the old downtown alleyways, curtains drawn, interrupted by the dim light of a pizzeria or the glow lamps of a kebab shop; the recycled barrels of a "wine bar," tapas. The post office, where employees are running around, chickens with their heads off, from counter to counter. The former reception halls of other public services, deserted, all lights out.

When I see Vincent again, he tells me this wasn't his world, their world, that nothing is familiar anymore, that he wishes he were thirty years older. He tells me he can't go to Marseille anymore, can't bear to see families, men, sleeping under porches, burned-out beggars, sick migrants, four-year-old kids with their hands out. I tell him about the bank employee in D., standing pregnant at her desk, wiped out by a white light, about-turning in her heels toward the boss's office. And then the graduating students, oriented to the computer, with only a rare few getting their preferred placement; and meanwhile others are waiting. Are made to wait. *Discouraging*. Keyword for our years. In May 2021, I send Joseph his passage from this book to look over. He talks, talks about the students, talks about the news of the day, he asks me whether I thought the swim was in the right place—I was still not sure of where to put it—the photos from the time at a local swimming hole, Nelly naked and some younger people, under the cover of vegetation back then, and the cops during the crime scene visit *hurry hurry* and cut it back for visibility from the road, and then Joseph starts talking about how things are nowadays, about the instant parties thrown during Covid abstinence and about the police who would come and lock the kids up, when he suddenly lowers his mask and says: *But why don't they revolt?*

I pick up the newspaper: Arseguel is dead. Shit. I expect to find several lines, but no. Just his death notice, in the obits of *La Provence*. I carefully read through all the names, all the first names of the children, the grandchildren, the sister . . . Before he died, had he asked that they leave out his writing? His being a poet (having assumed the mantle)? He did however just put out a book.*

---

* Gérard Arseguel (1938–2020), *Le Campanile de Sambuco* [The Campanile of Sambuco] (Éditions Larifla !, 2019).

Afterwards we talk about the local elections in D., about the forced and photocopied optimism of flyers, far-right-right-center-left. I'd just read this sentence in *La Petite Ville*,* by Chauvier, in reference to a mayor: "His optimism is consistent, apparently rooted in the order of things. Except that the order of things no longer appears practicable."

As for Lélen and his What do you think you're doing here, he tells me it doesn't surprise him, nor does Béa's correction. Sure, it makes us happy to see people who aren't from around here, and at the same time, what keeps you here?

Lélen used to be both very attached to D., and a pessimist, is what Béa told me, I tell Vincent. And then she was also amused by the fact that I wrote Lélun (in the first version of the text), that I hadn't differentiated between the two "in," like all Parisians, and how it included a joke, a regional joke, that played on the two "ins," which Parisians didn't get. Can you give me an example—how are the two "in" different? All right, Béa tells me, "in" pronounced like the number 1 [œ̃], and "in" as in "fin" /ɛ̃/, end of story.

Then; Vincent takes a photo from his backpack, four photos, rather, from a photo booth: four shots of the same two faces, happy and laughing, leaning against each other, of him and Patrick. I look for Patrick's features in this twenty-year-old. Vincent finally sets it straight:

---

* Éric Chauvier, *La Petite Ville* [The Town] (Collection L'ordinaire du capital, Éditions Amsterdam, 2017).

the record he never gave back to me, back then, wasn't *Ummagumma*, it was *Atom Heart Mother*.* Be sure to tell him.

\*

The tract *D. Deux Mains* (in reality, a half-dozen crowded A4 pages) tackles head-on and in great detail all that had been avoided when talking about D. at the time (as for writing about it . . .): the Cavallero affair, summed up as a "banal moral affair"; the "manipulation of opinion and repression"; drugs; homosexuality; the sexuality of minors. In the midst of a lively discussion with Dany, yesterday, Cathy, who first lived with Lélen for six years, remembers that there were shouting matches over the title, that she'd wanted *D. Putain*, that it would've better matched the content. Forty-five years later, Dany picks up the argument: it was too violent, it would have alienated folks, would have isolated them. *D. Putain* was better, Cathy reiterates.

The cops had driven up to the shed in the wake of the tract's dissemination and its ensuing scandal. They had searched the library, looking for drugs—but Lélen smoked only pipe—had hauled them off, him, for forty-eight hours in custody; her, they had released soon after: she was asthmatic, which was the reason she happened to land in D. in the first place, on the day of her

---

\* Pink Floyd, *Ummagumma* (1969), *Atom Heart Mother* (1970).

twentieth birthday, with her sister, in a Citroën 2CV, straight from Versailles, because they'd been told how breathable the air was. The tract, she says, we wrote in one night: it was born of the need to leave this unbearable world for good—to start all over.

Stephen sat down, in silence, on this afternoon for scattering ashes.

All of us were sitting or standing there, at the edge, when the terrain begins to palpably slope toward Lélen and Béa's house, now their children and grandchildren's, when it hurls itself into the valley from a standing start, in this landscape of soft curves, faraway rugged mountains, hardy flora, boxwoods and strawberry trees, little or withered trees, buzzing sounds and dry heat as early as February, on up into the diaphanous sky.

Patrick, who went to look for Cathy—I didn't dare speak to her and this wasn't the moment (Cathy: The right moment never comes, so better start now)—Patrick slowly raises the question of utopia. Cathy thinks they lived through the final utopia, that there will be no more utopias, that the world as it is and because of where it's headed cannot endure another. I react, I work up from the Peasant War, at the start of the sixteenth century, from Müntzer's article/letter,* from its radical return to primitive Christianity which demands the equality of all, the defeat and withdrawal of those in power, princes,

---

\* See Maurice Pianzola, *Thomas Munzer ou la Guerre des paysans* [Thomas Müntzer or the Peasants' War], reissued by Héros-limite, Geneva, 2015.

and the pope, the uprising to bring it about and for the castles to burn from northern Germany, where Béa was born, all the way to Austria, *via* Alsace and Lorraine, that there have always been sects, ever since the days of the apostles, to take these ideas up again, Hussites, Joachimites, then later in other ways communists and anarchists living in little communities for weeks, for months at a time, in Brussels, Barcelona, or in Latin America, wherever, and how it's like a pearl necklace with a shorter or longer chronological distance between strands but the pearl always comes back around—and how can you imply to Stephen, who is thirty, that it's all over? I understand the word *fatigue*, when one's been involved in the struggle for years, but don't speak to me of failure: we're on the rebound.

The difference with Müntzer and the others, says Cathy, is that it was never about religion . . . Not even forms of . . . spirituality? I ask . . . No, says Patrick. And to that end we would not bend. It was a political utopia without transcendence.

And, forcefully, he leans forward, articulating each word: No Gods. No masters.

Descending again into the valley, Patrick explains to me that, in those days, to go up to one's fixed-up shed was *to dwell out of step*.

Now that sense of time is no longer available to me, except in condensed form.

So two really important details you have to keep in mind, Stephen says as I sit down at the computer: the delightful taste of the first radishes that Cathy ate just after arriving from Versailles, radishes grown here on manure and cow pies.

And the eucalyptus scent of the military tents they slept in, Lélen and her, when they showed up in Portugal in 1974, for the Carnation Revolution.

\*

Substantive, precise, the texts in the tract D. Deux Mains are the work of intellectuals—professors, students. But these are hometown intellectuals: the kids who gather at Le Grand Café. Françoise (from Mézel) was the only one to remind me of something that was well-known even in the late 1990s: D. was a real "intellectual center" in the '70s, due mainly to the Rencontres Cinéma. People would come from Aix, from Marseille, to see films and the invited filmmakers—Garrel, Bellochio, Duras . . . For Patrick, this prolific period lasted five years. The screenings continued, albeit less prestigiously, and contemporary art was added. As elsewhere in France and the world, as in Paris, there's no real public engagement with that kind of art, that kind of cinema, it being justified only by the demands of the economy (of tourism or the marketplace). In D.: so long as there is a need for tourism, so long as it is all there is to live on, the need for that kind of art also exists. The day that tourism is no longer needed and *is no longer imposed on us,* these films, these artists, which don't speak to us and are useless, will be gotten rid of. In the metropolises and among the grande bourgeoisie, where there's business to be done (actual business), of finance mingled with politics: ditto. I've always been struck by these people's "classical" taste, proof of their total lack of understanding of anything being written, being filmed, being made in general. They have no curiosity for it. It doesn't interest them. De Gaulle and his grotesque Latin. Pompidou and his impeccably bland poetry anthology. Macron who musses up his hair the moment he starts talking culture. Bernard Arnault and his invariable series of classics all established already a hundred years ago. Pinault, supposedly cleverer: established thirty years ago (Lavier, Curlet, Cattelan . . .). Using artists who no longer need them to justify bringing three quarters of the population to its knees.

One of the reasons for telling myself I would have to write this text and the final triggering factor, once I'd already abandoned the idea, is a meal with an old friend. It had been many years since we last saw each other, but when all outward signs of affinity are in agreement, the thought that we have each traveled the same path occurs and that wherever we meet we will understand one another without having to spell it out. Then, as things give way to dessert, she suddenly launches into a diatribe against the locals in town where she bought a house forty years ago, upon returning from Los Angeles: she doesn't give a shit about them because she does performances all over the place with her artist friends every summer and she ends on something like: *They won't be pushing us around anytime soon. That's something they'll have to get used to, one way or another.* I picture myself in villager's garb, wearing my dress with three underskirts, flanked by my sheepdog: I lob a Molotov cocktail at her fucking house, which goes up in flames.

We kiss goodbye and in the car, as I drive through the sublime backcountry, its gorges and valleys teeming with wolves and red oak, rivulets waiting only for a storm to drown you, I say to myself I will write it after all, this text, because I'm a lousy nobody and a suburbanite who picked up how to write on my own in order to, among other things, bring up to date what we would be better off not ignoring anymore.

That's what I was told though, over and over again, in my family, the humiliating journey up to Paris, the provincial accent that sticks to your tongue, the urge to leave the moment you arrive; how one clenches buttocks in order to eat while thinking only of getting the hell out. It took me a long time, a very long time, to understand—perhaps it was looking at those postcards, yellowed photos from the start of the century in which an old Auvergne native, cracked with wrinkles, leans against his hovel.

There is no nation. Just a pacification of the provinces.

## 4

But is that what's in one's head, at thirty-three, in the mid-'70s, after seven years at war now that one is starting to lose—the war? Over the phone, Marguerite repeats to me from Paris that what fundamentally drove Nelly was truth. There is something worse than having a bad thought, and that is having a ready-made thought: one of Nelly's phrases. Marguerite talks about her inability to conform, her unpredictable character, she scared people, this unyielding intellectual powerhouse, the moments she dropped by without notice, it was always the same, she came over for meals and then everyone talked politics, her physical side, athletic, strong, with dreams of single-handed sailing, her rapid-fire intellect, her excitement (her exuberance, says Vincent), which she shared with everyone equally, child, dog, adult.

Most of the local witnesses think X., the homosexual, cost her dear in the affair. Not Vincent: X. allowed her to take things even further in terms of *I don't give a shit what people in town think*, he tells me.

In fall 1976, she wins her defamation case against *Ici Paris*.

In the tract that caused a scandal (the charge of "public indecency through tract distribution"), Nelly adds a complementary text, the only one of hers I was able to read:

> THE FACTS
>
> Woman, 33 years old, no children, divorced, teaching high school Philosophy, with tenure, appointed last year, I have just been charged with "incitement of minors to debauchery" by an investigating judge.
>
> It is common knowledge that a condemnation for "indecency" results in permanent removal from the Éducation nationale.
>
> The probable motivations of this charge can be traced back to the spring of last year:
>
> 1) I expressed support for the lycée students' protest strike against the Haby reforms. The demonstration of stated support infringes upon a ministerial text which stipulates that every communication between students and teachers is forbidden within the premises (?).
>
> 2) I participated in the teachers' solidarity strike with the employees of PTT and the school workers—until the end.
>
> 3) As an active member of MLAC I tried—in vain—to organize a sex information program at the lycée, in keeping with ministerial instructions, and true to the question in its actual state among young people, a state which the practice of abortions at the MLAC has made us SEE.

4) I am the subject of an "investigation" requested by the university education board pursuant to an unknown student's parent's "complaint" concerning the learning objectives chosen for the *explication de texte* of an Antonin Artaud poem (in the curriculum) which concludes with the incriminating verse: "In a dead maid's cunt."

5) The lycée's principal told me at the beginning of that year that he knew I had said the curriculum was "shit," and I never said that.

6) Lastly, that year, among the comrades who were restoring a collective space, of which I was the owner, was S.D., a comrade like the rest of them. This young man had just been charged with indecent assault. The police had gained entry to the space twice without a search warrant, warning me they could enter wherever, whenever.

I was interrogated over the presumed fact that experiences of Love and exchanges of feelings between S.D. and young people may have occurred there in the space.

One thing is certain: if such acts took place, it is not for me to approve or disapprove of them. I was not there. I am not a boarding school supervisor. My doors are not locked. It must be for this that I have been charged.

*Nelly Cavallero*

Marguerite says her strongest position was this:

> I didn't do it.
> And regardless it's fine.

Nelly chose to finish by closing upon the question of private property—all the way to the bone.

In 1976, short sentences alluding to this litter the newspaper clippings of the politics section in D. The *Le Monde* journalist writes "the idea is spreading [. . .] a political operation seeking to discredit the municipality's socialist management style, just before the district elections [. . .]. The mayor takes a stance: 'D. is not a depraved town. The publicity endangering our town is abhorrent [. . .]. I am under the impression that the far left wants to take advantage of this affair to provoke an agitation.' Hélène corroborates this version with me: two commissioners who came up from Marseille for the investigation had the last word in all this: Madame, they said to Nelly, it's due to political reasons that don't involve you in the least.

The eternal problem: how to get rid of "leftists," radicals, those who are excitable, etc. Not numerous but boisterous. Chamayou, in his book, speaks of the same thing, on a much less local scale, in this same period: activist cells in the U.S. launching boycotts against several big enterprises (Shell, Union Carbide, Monsanto . . .). Since that seemed to have an impact, they turned their attention to the summits. As it happens, Chamayou stresses the summits' lack of inventiveness fairly often:

whether they used whitewashing (*greenwashing*, *pinkwashing*); the cudgel—or both.

After '68, in France, the summit opted for the cudgel, as did the Éducation nationale. It was Françoise (from Grenoble) who spoke to me about the book that came out on Maspero in 1972, *Repression in Education*, which she saw on display three years ago at an exhibition on the counterculture in France from 1970–1980—the vaunted private foundation near Bastille published a thick catalogue which I participated in for the occasion. In the Maspero book, Françoise's case took up four full pages with the insert title: *Repression and Sexual Education*.

*The facts* (the text begins):
— On March 19, 1971, an educational action committee distributes a tract in Grenoble that details the experiences of J. Celma.
— On March 26, 1971, Françoise C. and the students of her tenth-grade class discuss this text.
— On April 23, the director of the fédération Armand proposes to the administrative council that they deliberate over "the case of a colleague" (who would go unnamed that day) whose classroom conduct has been admonished.
— On May 11, Monsieur Vacheret, the inspector general called upon by the minister, arrives to inspect Françoise C., who then states she is unable to hold class as she usually would without a

preliminary (in-class) discussion. A "refusal to teach" is therefore not at issue.
— On May 29, Françoise C. is notified of her suspension with pay, etc.
— On October 12, the academic council declares her dismissal with a two-thirds majority, etc.

Françoise went looking in her archives for this old folder she had not once since stuck her nose in: a substantial batch of typewritten pages—letters from the Chief Commissioner of Security, an exchange between Françoise and her inspector, memorandum written by her in her own defense, mail from the parent-teacher association, letters of denunciation from parents (a jeweler, an associate professor), a letter from a student . . . The tract is barely even mentioned and sexuality was not really at issue: there were denunciations of noise in class, debates that were confusing, texts that weren't part of the curriculum (*Springtime in the Parking Lot* by Christiane Rochefort),* no final exam prep. I remember landing in the backwaters, in the mid-1990s, and how a student's mother admonished me in hushed tones for having her son's excellent ninth grade class read *Maigret and the Yellow Dog*.**

As one reads the long list of teachers who lost their licenses in 1970–1971 and the reasons for their being

---

\* Christiane Rochefort, *Printemps au parking* (Éditions Grasset, 1969).
\*\* Georges Simenon, *Le Chien jaune* (Éditions Fayard, 1931).

pulled, the institutional admonishments in summary take the form of: they spoke up; they taught students; they were poorly dressed.

I didn't see any comments about their hair, and yet Patrick told me that hair was a key factor and grounds for constant humiliation—dirty faggot, you're disgusting, go wash up, cut your hair, etc. N.G. described how she would walk around barefoot in Aix in the late '80s, but didn't mention being given any shit for it. Whatever the case, in our neck of the woods, hippie-bashing survived all the trends and even punks were seen as hippies.

In all this denunciation mail there are letters through which the anger and fear of the good parents comes to expression, who see the outrages of May '68 and another world encroach on *their home*, the good school in their respectable town. Some of the parts I copy out for you: [. . .] a teacher who has seduced them, by which I mean, has led them astray [. . .] <u>A line has been crossed.</u> This was a work of destruction and "disorder"[. . .] an insult to liberty [. . .] a complaint against a twisted teacher who is ruining our children for life [. . .] a dishonest and lecherous teacher [. . .] tolerated inside the equally pernicious and vulgar institutions of learning [. . .]scandalous activities such as these [. . .] blatantly obvious that this person has lost it [. . .] a psychological examination is called for [. . .] A detoxified educational system seems unforeseeable [. . .] though on the other hand a posture of systematic denigration of the family is the everlasting rule [. . .] I demand such a person be stripped of their license, mere transfer to some other district is no solution, etc.

Françoise held onto the minutes of a class council meeting on that famous tenth-grade class with whom she discussed the Celma tract. Therein I discover that the class council as we know it now dates back to September 1970. What did they have before? I guess the institution of the class council was viewed as progress. There are parent representatives, after all, and student representatives, delegates (which date back to 1969). A classic debriefing on a class of troublemakers is what I would call it, with my present-day teacher's eyes: [. . .] no sense of grammar [. . .] in an atmosphere like that [. . .] impossible to carry on with all the noise, says the English teacher. Impossible to hold class in silence, say the Spanish and History teachers. And then, of course, there are the usual yea-sayers, in Physics and Math in this case, who claim that for them things couldn't be going any better, that they have no complaints when it comes to students not paying attention, and that it might be due to the subject matter (rigor, order and discipline of the sciences vs the load of nonsense known as the liberal arts—and underlying this, the incompetency of one's colleagues, who cannot *hold* a totally holdable class themselves: the debriefing of teachers who are average, servile, and snitches all at once). Except that this detailed report is from a girls' class at an excellent lycée in Grenoble, the lycée of the bourgeoisie.

Who were these girls of 1971, difficult characters who

loudly disrupted class with questions (says the English teacher)? What did they want? What did they desire? Did they have any expectations whatever of the institution? Not the bac diploma, obviously, which they seemed not very concerned about that year. Before the meeting, the two class reps had decided to refuse to speak about any disciplinary measures in the name of reaching an agreement with all of their classmates, according to the report. This pure refusal still puts them within the orbit of the great refusal of '68 as regards authority: they won't speak about it—accepting that to speak about it confirms one's ability to do so, so then it is negotiable. It's participation in the circus.

Self-discipline (the word was still in use when I was a middle schooler), this would not work within a structure which is itself disciplinary as a whole (buildings, schedules, calls . . . framing of time and space, full framing).

Recently I had a conversation with a friend and colleague trying to arrange her class another way—a reading corner, students in groups of twos and threes, learning together . . . But in the class before hers, they were scratching away on their own and passing notes on the sly, and what is both implicitly and explicitly promoted by everyone (parents, teachers, administration, all of society), is an instructor who keeps a tight rein on the class, so those who try another way don't carry much weight, are buried in the noise (this is the cool class where one can relax and take revenge for one's own troubles or the problems of others).

The recent fiction film shot in Montfermeil, in la cité

des Bosquets,* places poor kids and adults under the supervision of indisputable masters (such as a big brother, religious leader or delinquent boss, and of course the police—I understand their raising hell at school! It's the one place they can). The conclusion one then draws from all this, Paris-banlieue, countryside-mountains, is that what people want is authority—it is what they know: either shut the hell up or raise hell; heads or tails. Who wants autonomy? Who knows what that is, how to put it together and organize it? In their current state, our institutions will not teach us. Since institutional critique in action doesn't work (i.e., they fire you unless you leave on your own), we suggest you'd do better to rethink the relationships within the institution, that is, work in teams and play nice.

All one agrees upon with any certainty (including among teachers) is that what students will retain (will not forget) are the outings and invited speakers. Let me think, what did I retain, me, whose memory is not great, from my school years—what shines through? In middle school, Barjavel,** who came and visited our library; and a play, *The Good Person of Szechwan*,*** which we went to see by bus at the other end of the suburb. What I made in arts and crafts. And then the faces of my teachers, the likable ones. Who will realize the enormity of the thing, that what remains, luminously, of school, are

---

* Ladj Ly, *Les Misérables* (2019).
** René Barjavel (1911–1985), author of, among others, *La Nuit des temps*, published in English as *The Ice People* in the 1970s.
*** A play by Bertolt Brecht.

the moments we weren't there, moments not at school, that didn't look like it? But organized by school. Is the affectionate interest of a few teachers' measurable?

I offered a final essay topic from the early 2000s to my ninth-graders, a subversive text that had gone missing somewhere between Giono and Le Clézio: the main character, Josyane, who is fifteen, refuses to respond to the guidance counselor, who makes her take tests and bores her to death with her well-intended questioning (example: "Do you like the countryside?"). "I didn't see why it was necessary to rack one's brain just to choose ahead of time what sort of box one will be forced to sweat in," thinks Josyane. The girls of 1971 would have been quick on the uptake (incidentally, the text dates from 1969, excerpted from *Petits enfants du siècle* (*Little Children of the Century*), by Christiane Rochefort). The girls of 2019 ask questions; perhaps they understood.

Whether it's 1971 or 2019, the side of power puts forward the same arguments in the same way (but we for sure put ours forward with a repertoire that was partly in use in the early '70s): *students have to be able to study and teachers to teach*—a play on words that shuts down every discussion by turning a tautology into a truth—"common sense," the first sense to arise when one isn't thinking. In 1971, Gaxotte of the Académie française expounds: "The real question is simply whether *all* of the builders of the New University wish to see their students finding employment. Even disregarding the rowdier ones, are there not many who long to mass-produce the perpetually unemployed who then transform naturally into seditionists all on their own?"

Unemployment does not even register where reduced hours have already done the trick, and this (other) evidence: school is preparation for the labor market and thus finding one's place in *society,* all other forms of social organization being, by choice: excluded, inadmissible, unthinkable.

Stéphane often told me that when he was young, at seven or eight, it used to make him anxious to think he might not pass the bac and thus not find a wife. *Society* being what it is, one's fear of being in it should be at least equivalent to the anguish of one's exclusion from it.

Gaxotte, in his phrasing, has ambitions for us: he sees *seditionists* (magnificent word and it anchors itself there and then to the seriousness of history) where everyone has already fled or run off. Innumerable films of the era, and the most beautiful ones, follow characters who go away—one has the right to go away, says Baudelaire. Up until 1973, at least, they go away, with nothing, at times a small bag—that's the ending of *Who Cares: Anatomy of a Delivery Boy*, by Claude Faraldo, in the early morning light of the world to come which is everything except for the one we know. The teen in *Springtime in the Parking Lot* leaves home when his father tells him to stop blocking the TV.

We're not quite there yet, though we have broken new ground since four years ago: the Nuit debout assemblies were already no longer directed at elected representatives. The Yellow Vests didn't negotiate; their ephemeral associations, their wildcat blockades, their non-organization in a way helped them achieve nearly everything they set out to do. Will the tightening of control measures for which Covid is the pretext take us even further?

There would be three solutions: first, overhauling the institutions; second, leaving the city to create communes, zones to defend; third, doing both (which takes lots of people, and energy to boot). Mornings, I lean into the first, afternoons into the third, and evenings into the second. Or even . . . ?

\*

It's about controlling (what my father used to call "drilling," but that grates our ears, which we prefer to caress with words like "assisting," "supporting") the youth.

Rather than allow their children to get away from them, the parents of 1968 preferred to adopt what only two months prior had been deemed an intolerable laxness, scandalous "liberties"—the right to abortion was made acceptable finally because Simone Veil asserted it; the age of majority at eighteen, but not until 1974 under Giscard.

Caught between the need to not cut oneself off from the changing times or from one's children and those keeping an eye on them in spite of it all—which turns into keeping an eye on the teaching they provide—

the parent-teacher association that denounces Françoise skates around the subject: the "participation promised in May '68," yes, but the "type of culture proposed" by these new teachers, no; "this resistance to change which holds us hostage," no, but "these attempts of wild pedagogy," no; conclusion: "the structures of teaching itself" must be revised. "Structure" is of interest here (it's a word that often gets repeated nowadays like a mantra every time children or the we in general is the topic, and then we're thought of as children or immature beings, to whom everything has to be explained endlessly over and over again which is about "structuring" or channeling behaviors). Whereas "structure" is naturally opposed to "amorphous," it isn't to "another form." But what instructor, what father-mother, what decision-maker, would not prefer seeing their children amorphous rather than in a form not their own? It's more about pointing out the *or* (*or* the structure *or* the amorphous) than repressing an excluded third: another form, other forms of life are possible. The evidence was brought (recalled) in 1968.

In 1971, Françoise discovers that teachers are always dubbed over by their file. A file of which there is no knowledge and to which access will likely never be granted in full. In order to complete the personal documents she sent me in the mail, she goes to the archives at the Board of Education, which prevaricates, just can't be bothered or find the time, doesn't intend to deliver the breakdown of an old case however administratively pathetic: in her defense, in September 1971, she noted a list of irregularities that cover two A4 pages and then some. In summary, it's a mess—bits and pieces left and right, mixed together, photocopied superfluously (she for example points out the presence of "press clippings" that were completely out of place in an official file). I sometimes asked myself what my own file might hold, me whose attitude had long been one of discretion bordering on evanescence, that is, mistrust approaching paranoia—why would this institution, which has shown itself historically capable of dismissing and laying off part of its staff *in dürftiger Zeit*\* without suffering any consequences become so tolerant overnight? Have they noticed that I started publishing books and that, as need be, I was able to come and rifle through their shelves, their files, their forgotten or stashed away boxes, their O.S.T.s and their laws, to retranscribe conversations, from Board of Trustee meetings, about class and discipline, instances of overstep, gestures, looks. *Wozu Dichter?* Well, this, for one. This is what they're for.

    Françoise, who had no idea what was and wasn't allowed when she entered the Éducation nationale right at the start of the 1970s, discovered that they considered her a *leader*. But there are no leaders in the Éducation nationale in 1971: it's the years 1971, 1972, 1973 that lead. The high-water mark of the high school students'

---

\* "Wozu Dichter in dürftiger Zeit?" (What use are poets in times of need?) writes Hölderlin in "Bread and Wine" (1800).

movement lasted from 1971 to 1973, which included segments of the eighth- and ninth-graders and even middle school students, without even mentioning vocational education. In June 1971, exclusionary measures were taken against hundreds of high schoolers, entire classes were emptied from one school year to the next to undermine contestation. The heart of the high schoolers' expectations: to put an end to authority as practiced since the introduction of schooling (children of the '50s, the post-war years, that is), a.k.a. authoritarian authority. Page 111 of the Maspero book: "High school was considered the enclosure to which neither politics nor violence should gain admittance. But for the defenders of order, after May '68, there remained only one means of preventing politics from entering the schools, and that was violence. At Collège-lycée Jacques-Decour, it was the non-violent administration that sequestered a high schooler in order to hand him over to the police; at Reuil, the superintendent slapped a student, called the police, reported the "agitators," collaborated with the repression. On January 13, in Grenoble, a student of the Jean-Bart lycée was condemned to four months in prison, of which two were a suspended sentence, in secret proceedings in children's court, for having written political slogans on the school walls."

The film seen yesterday depicts today's high schoolers replaying scenes from workers' revolts drawn from '70s documentaries perfectly.* When the filmmaker, in the teacher's position, asks them what they know about politics, what a union is, they say nothing, flounder, fumble for words—they have restaged the scenes, affectingly, superbly, but do not understand them. At the end, the high schoolers replay the scene from Mantes 2019—one class, with hands on their heads, on their knees, some faced up against the wall, before of cops who film and heckle them: "Now here's a class that knows how to behave!" It's not the scene, or the restaging that persuades them to blockade their school building, but a classmate's detention for a tag. Filmed in front of school, they no longer perform.

    I was born into the oft-repeated idea that schools and universities were "sanctuaries," sacred enclosures the police would never penetrate. Regularly the police show evidence to the contrary and are happy doing so. They walk right into the rural middle school where I work like they own the place, keeping up conversations with the administration, teaching classes on drugs—I rarely take any drugs and everything I know about getting high is from this one policeman, who comes around every year to see the eighth-graders, who has taught me, in the most cutting-edge terms, about how they are made, their effects, and the penalties prescribed by law which he announces with relish at the end of the hour

---

* Jean-Gabriel Périot, *Nos défaites* [Our Defeats] (2019). In Mantes-la-Jolie, in late 2018, high schoolers were forced onto their knees, their hands on their heads.

just before recess. His class always holds the students' full attention. The classes for *sexual information* that volunteers hold, however, with their interminable list of every kind of harassment and violence, are met with much yawning, slouching, slumping forward; I tap one of my good students on the elbow that he might politely ask at least one question before the bell rings.

One of the first times of late I heard about the police entering and clubbing people at a college, I was alarmed (just like the first time a disabled person in a wheelchair was clubbed, the same with an old lady, a kid, or the patrons of a bar sitting around a patio table: 2018–2019; today, January 29, 2020, I'm no longer astonished at the CRS having thrown stun grenades and teargas canisters into the entryway of a preschool, in Paris, in the 12th arrondissement.


But the Maspero book teaches me that university police forces—security guards—were created the day after 1968. Speaking of students: "They either shape up or get shipped out," says Pompidou in June 1971. And there was that young guy, too, whose mouth was torn off by a shot at point-blank range (which I'll come back to later). The state's rhetoric and its implementation always seems to come back fresher than ever with something totally new that's never been seen before. "Nouvelle société" is what Pompidou-Marcellin designated the return to moral order that clubs people on the head or lifts girls up by their hair, like the principal of that CET (collège d'enseignement technique, a vocational middle school). It's bizarre now to think that for years (or decades as far as I'm concerned) we took for granted that the state by and large wanted the best for us, or at least it didn't wake up each and every morning with the thought of boot-stomping us into the ground and taking out an eye.

If I took too much time deciding to write this text, it's because it felt like a distant time, telling us little or speaking through gauze, with its teachers who gave everyone crap and were pissed off about some tract or birth control pills, its barefooted hippies who were insulted as queers—meanwhile there was AIDS, September 11, the fall of the wall, Islamists, gay marriage. Eras are incomparable. Analogy is a mistake. In using the past as a starting point, one understands the present poorly, even if the past can only be understood by starting from the present. But am I trying too hard to understand? Things crop up—glimpses, snatches. I copy them down, I record them. I really would like to know if you all see what I see, if you hear what I hear, whether you think I'm exaggerating or falling short of reality.

# 5

Françoise (from Grenoble) tells me about an issue of *Tout!* the police would have confiscated from her home as evidence. I imagine it somehow relates to the *We want everything!* of those years, which a book by Nanni Balestrini, the Italian poet and founding member of Potere Operaio,* had as its title (a PDF of the book is easily found on the internet). She tells me *Tout!* was the newspaper of VLR, Vive La Révolution, the Mao-Spontex group.

Online I click into their scanned issues, mauves and yellows, greens and blues. I see a note being passed with the title in a clumsy, childish handwriting: *I would like to kiss a girl on her ass* . . . the sentence that took down Celma, the elementary school teacher! Among what was made public, of the children's was also this: "If you see a wounded master, finish him off!" which the Comité d'Action Enseignants had adapted for their tract which they distributed near the exit of Françoise's school: "If you see a wounded teacher, finish him off! . . ."

Two years later, in 1973, the filmmaker Claude Faraldo released *Themroc*, in which the characters end

---

* The Italian organization Workers' Power (1967–1973). Toni Negri was one of its leading figures.

up scarfing (eating) cops (arms, thighs) after they kill them. I keep seeing more and more of these kinds of cannibalistic phrases these last few months. Z. tells me about their savagery in Paris, on a Saturday, in the well-heeled neighborhoods: ladies behind a store window; Z. and their buds, girls and guys, press their wide-open, starving, salivating mouths up against the glass. The ladies beat a hasty retreat. Shall we eat the rich?

The Comité d'Action Enseignants' tract was just sent to me by Françoise, after rediscovering it finally in her archives—missing piece and centerpiece, whose discussion had been proposed by her students in class and which cost her, I stress, her job. It's three densely typed A4 sheets—so, to call the six A4 pages of *D. Deux mains* a tract was neither a mistake nor an exception (we, on the other hand, we'll call a meager A5 with ten phrases in 36 font a tract in the hope that people will have the patience to read it).

The tract opens with the revelation that the Éducation nationale hired large numbers of replacements in the days following 1968, elementary school replacements. After a half-day training session, Celma lands in a mixed-age classroom of students who were between nine and eleven, which was already outside the norm: "I was dropped into a class that had been applying Rogers' non-directivity." I look up who or what this Rogers is: originally a therapist, he valued personal experience above all else. The children that Celma is supposed to "assist" already work on their own "without my giving them any instructions in the least," they begin with arithmetic, correct their own work, copy down the answers, then French, and onto whatever comes next . . . They teach him the method, teach him the trade. All worked up, and probably also annoyed at having noticed he wasn't doing all that much for them at the end of the day, Celma decides to take the experiment even further (which wasn't one for the kids: just their way of working) by eliminating all directivity, all discipline, all moral censure. In short, he regains control. When they start drawing wee-wees and hoo-has, it was proof of child sexuality for Celma—he himself acknowledges he hasn't read much (not much Freud, anyway). He closes with several sharp phrases: "Teachers, you're castrating your students," "If you're a teacher, you're a dirty cop," etc.

That's how I read the tract, at a fifty years' distance—did the girls of 1971 come up with the same questions, the same conclusions? Were they more understanding of Celma than I am? Were they shocked?

\*

What remains with me of the other Françoise (from Mézel) is the radiant memory of someone still *living* another way of teaching, someone impassioned by pedagogy whose only worry is that children might be unhappy learning (she corrects: might be unhappy coming to school). She describes a young girl she once knew, who started out in a Steiner kindergarten, the welcome songs, the dances, the cabin constructions and the looms that prepared them for reading and writing, which they didn't start doing until they were seven. Then when she moved on to first grade, she grew a tougher exterior, she was paler (these are Françoise's words).

Are there colors for her? Is she playing? Is she laughing? Françoise asks. Are we still able to ask ourselves these sorts of questions, parents and teachers, after the children have been sent to school? The Waldorf-Steiner children who enter the school system don't understand at first: the other students don't know how to make anything with their hands. Freinet, Ferrer*—or Bellenger's educational project during the Paris Commune—that's what it is: *integral* teaching: "Every worker, everyone employed in physical labor should be equipped to write a book, with feeling and talent, without leaving their job."**

Later on, Hélène will correct: careful, Steiner's pedagogy has dubious origins, with fascist roots . . . Possibly. It depends of course on the application.

Françoise is confident: for her, we are in a slow revolution. Uninterrupted since '68. We are in the waves, waves of coming to consciousness, and young people, today, they are getting out of the system, building new schools

---

* Francisco Ferrer (1859–1909), libertarian pedagogue, founder of the *Modern School*.
** Henri Bellenger, *Le Vengeur* [The Avenger], "L'enseignement professionnel et intégral" [Professional and integral teaching], May 7, 1871.

(she cites several examples in the area), she talks about self-managed farms, with off-grid water and electricity.

What's different post-'68, is work. That what was to be done was nothing, that work was participation, was cultivated, carried over. Not in an office, not in the Éducation nationale—not in a profession with the aim of changing nothing, transforming nothing, making nothing. But now all career paths are possible.

She remembers the string of years when they, the children of May, wanted to live off nothing, to go to the caves, caves hermits lived and still live in, both summer and winter, an hour away from me, in the mountains. A woman, Catholic, elderly. They would climb up to bring her food, wood to keep warm. She never came down. She was a healer, too. This was in the 1990s. Her order (the order is always on the hermit's case) eventually succeeded in getting her to come down, then stuck her in a convent, far away, in Normandy or something like that. But she couldn't bear confinement. So, they found her a cabin, a shelter at the edge of the garden. Which is where she died.

\*

In the issue of *Tout!* I scroll on the screen, Celma takes up much less space than a photograph of Richard Deshayes, face riddled with blood—no eyes, no nose.

It was taken at a demo. He's leaning over to help a girl off the ground. A cop takes aim with a grenade launcher and shoots him point-blank in the face. The splinters cut out his right eye, cut off his nose, shatter his jaw. Deshayes collapses. Immediately, other cops throw themselves on top of him and beat him with vicious kicks.

The newspaper published this poem:

> Fourteen wounded at a demonstration,
> It's happened before: the cops hit hard,
> We strike back.
> But a twenty-year old comrade
> Was disfigured for life by
> Law enforcement
> Professionals, certified meat-packers
> Trained and worked up for the
> Kinds of operations
> That Richard Deshayes took in the face
> A grenade shot at point-blank range, Claudine is
> Seriously wounded in the
> Throat, the same way.
> And others too.
> To aim, shoot, kill.
> To do it
> One has to want it.
> He lost an eye,
> It was organized;
> The special units,
> They know what they do:
> Hours and hours
> Of daily training
> With what in their head:

Suppress, shatter, break; choke
Hold, contain, maintain Order
And with whom in their head: the rioter
the outlaw, the extremist on both sides [...]
This too, to do it
One has to want it.
One has to plan, dare, decide, prepare.
The creation of a "special force"
Of police is a plan
A long-term plan
With months of studies, surveys, and
Training, a material adapted
To new and particular forms of struggle,
The French bourgeoisie sees its future
As bleak.
They are right to. [...]
In no other period of its history
has capitalism had as much trouble
Legitimating its own existence;
Everything it has built requires
Conclusion outside
Its own limits.
It cannot suppress the hope for another society
In the name of a present:
Which calls for it everywhere.
The temporary takes hold,
Exasperation becomes routine.
No one knows anymore where there is Order
The stalled society of '71 can't even
Make the reforms

That would allow them to
Legitimate the suppression
"While awaiting improvement."
The only assurance one gives oneself is
A solid rampart of oppression
That grows with each passing year.
And how they eat it up, the dogs!
In terms of planning,
It's the only thing
They can guarantee.
They show too
That they foresee even more violent
Protest taking shape,
They are right again.
This still dispersed,
Still disparate force
Proceeds both in the sterile irruption
Of the angry racegoers at Vincennes
And the workers' assemblies like
The one this week at Renault-Flins,
Of the 14,000 suicides per year
Like a delinquency
That is no longer containable
In the expansion of porn
As in the WLM.
It may take a long time to find herself
An identity in a barely coherent
Radical critique or to articulate projects
Based on still marginal
Aspirations and dreams.

She can't be wrong.
They know it.
It's against this force
That thousands of energies are nonetheless
Organized to destroy
All that rises which is resistant
Creative, generous.
In anticipation of necessary assassinations
To maintain Order.
We must spy on them
Study them, undermine them,
Attack them, destroy them.
Everyone will pitch in in their own way.
We will gain power over our lives
by bringing down the power of death.
WATCH THE POLICE!


I remember a Louis Malle film shot in Paris in the early '70s.* Planted with his sound man on the sidewalks, he asks passersby questions, questions about their life, life in general. The times are rough. I used to picture these days as high-spirited, lustrous, a child on vacation by the sea, in Argelès, on the Plage des Pins, right by the discotheque whose façade had the black psychedelic silhouette of a longhaired girl with a nice twerking butt. But in Malle's film, the times are rough. People are depressed,

---
\* *Place de la République* (1974).

seemingly loaded down with extra baggage. Nonetheless, I'm happy to see the old dark streets of Paris I remember from childhood, the bistros, and only a few boutiques.

I rediscovered Deshayes in a short documentary* dating from 2017 where he's walking and talking on a beach holding closely on to a friend's guiding arm: "What the grenade offered me was a diamond in a ghostly pale jewel box, he says, the diamond is the feeling that one part of your being will remain unaffected by whatever might happen, whether richer or poorer . . . masculine or feminine, Jew or Arab." He speaks of his youth as a blend of shame and influence, of the movie *Easy Rider*, which showed them the possibility of another life and how the best thing to do was to bring one's own life to the revolution. "The content of revolution is the content of people's lives. So yes, he says, there's so much that's more important than grinding away, growing old, not getting cancer and consuming . . . But what's most important is for you to know what that is. How do you really want to live? What do you want for yourself? For a life that looks like you?"

---

* Frédéric Loth, *Les Ombres et la Lumière* [Shadows and Light] (2017).

# 6

I cite films . . . But all Françoise (from Grenoble), Marguerite, or Gilberte speak of is theater, all they resonate with is theater—and Nelly, who married a set designer, lived both with and without him her whole life. For the girls of 1971—or of 1962 until 1967, the years they studied at the École Normale Supérieure of Fontenay, finishing first in class (Françoise), and third (Nelly)—Politics and Theater, one and the same. Françoise tells the story about how she went to great lengths to bring Armand Gatti to her school, how Gatti was important. Or even Jean-Baptiste Thiérrée in *Le Chevalier au pilon flamboyant* (*The Knight of the Burning Pestle*), from 1607, republished by Stock in 1971 in their series "Théâtre ouvert":

> Now, Fortune, if thou be'st not only ill,
> Show me thy better face, and bring about
> Thy desperate wheel, that I may climb at length
> And stand. This is our place of meeting,
> If love have any constancy. Oh, age,
> Where only wealthy men are counted happy!
> How shall I please thee? How deserve thy smiles,
> When I am only rich in misery?

I ask Françoise if she knew anything about the troupe Nelly joined after D. and the pulling of her license, or suspension rather, by the Éducation nationale: Attroupement. Attroupement is at the heart of the writer's book, in which Nelly, under a nickname, is one of the characters. It didn't ring a bell. Her director (or guide or guru, at the time) would go on to become quite famous.

What happened is that, after D., Nelly went to Avignon (a three-hour drive) for the festival, and then followed the troupe on to Strasbourg where she was in residence at TNS (National Theatre of Strasbourg).

Nowadays when you have a residency (Thank god, I can afford to refuse: I have my civil servant's salary to live on), at first you're happy, because it requires many pulled strings or an established reputation to get one; then, since you know you won't get much work done at your residency, you finish what you still have to do at home before you leave, so you can fully commit yourself to the instructional workshops, activities in the schools, the middle schools, the high schools, presentation of your work, show opening-closing, photos with electeds. Two years ago, we were, Antoine, Christian, and I, each of us from a different generation, received at a castle for a reading; over dinner the question concerning residencies was put to us and how one might go about setting one up in this castle, at some later date, what the writers would do while there. The three of us, in unison, replied: Nothing! We all agreed without first talking it over.

People always ask why you became a writer, teacher, this, that, the other. Writer or teacher, to be left the hell alone. Since we can't avoid work altogether, let it at least be a grind where you're left the hell alone as much as possible. But even those jobs, where they used to leave you the hell alone as much as possible, have been overtaken by deranged interventionism, assignments, evaluations, requests; the moment you are just about to start, something always comes up to tap you on the shoulder and draw your attention elsewhere, confusing productivism with hyperactivity. To find the time, the precious few hours you are able to write, i.e., be left alone, you must clear everything that hinders you out of the way.

The writer, in this book from 1978 that precedes his regionalist period and in which he tells the story of Attroupement (he was there with Nelly), has some straightforward sentences about work, such as: "Still, a society where people who work with their hands see themselves as losers is a society which ought to die."


So, the guide or guru, his troupe Attroupement, flanked by Nelly and the writer, having left Avignon, arrive in Strasbourg. The work—performing; actors perform— was always a stand-in, back then, for what could be grandly pronounced "institutional analysis," a form of attempted subversion, or at least contestation, of the institution (TNS—Théatre Nationale de Strasbourg, in this case). For example, there was a great argument about smoking on stage or in the auditorium. Of course, it drives the fire department crazy, but then again, in the discussion over smoking and whether it's part of the actor's performance, and how if the actor is smoking in a scene, it remains unclear why the spectator shouldn't be permitted to smoke in the auditorium under the pretext they weren't performing, and in 1976, at any event, this didn't strike people as an inappropriate or far-fetched debate. But since they discuss everything at length, they don't perform much; and since they don't perform much, they're on edge; some of them ship out, though on the whole the guide or guru keeps a firm grip on things. The troupe is a community. Theater is living in community. No distinctions between art and life.

But what was the relationship like with those who were not in the troupe, not involved in that life? Barmaids, the writer writes, feel as though they are despised, "they spit *Attroupement* out with venom, its leftism and its begging." And they do keep asking for money to buy themselves sandwiches. Their poverty, since they make theater, excuses their arrogance. In light of what they do and moreover who they are, they should be rich, but they're not, so they make others pay.

A kind of cunning, or ingenuity, rather, related to the question of money (public or private) remains unchanged: We don't turn down money (from the state), we want "a polemical and problematic use of money," is how the writer recaps the group's approach. The reason you have to pay us (and well, at that) is that we are in a position to be discussing this question (arguing, debating, performing). So it's only right for those without the means, time, or inclination to debate or perform it, to also be paid less.

From the periphery, both the writer and Nelly observe this, caustically. Shortly thereafter, the former, back in the sticks, launches his career as a popular novelist, rooted in the region, as they say nowadays, and forever bitter.

There's a sentence of Nelly's which the writer recalls in his 1978 book that I don't understand: "There's a power structure, and every position of contestation in relation to it is null and void." Further on, he says she says: "I'm in a conflictual situation with power, whatever it may be." Does she mean that all attacks on an institution (even "from within") are doomed to failure, and that that's precisely why we can only want to attack it? Is she implying that we are doomed to the institutionalization of even the least institutionalizing of institutions—such as emancipated schools, self-managed communities—that turn their assemblies into routines in the long term and contemplate on perpetuating their future excellence? And since this is how it is, all positions of contestation are null and void when their institutionalization is baked in from the start.

No. I don't see myself thinking this. The institution is a mold they pour us into. It's founded by them for us to be poured into. If it makes life unbearable—and making life unbearable is what's specified in its charter, its institutional habits—due to the fact it holds on to power and is unable to let up, at the risk of growing weak or falling apart, then there's nothing left for us but to destroy it or leave it. Nothing, no institution, power, established fact, rules, or even laws, should make more than a single life unbearable.

The guide or guru, who had been a teacher, gives up Attroupement in 1982, directs a national drama center in 1986, is then a university professor; thesis directed by Balibar, Derrida, Lacoue-Labarthe, and others. As an old man, he's still a handsome guy. Did Nelly bang him? The book doesn't say.

*It's said one changes institutions by entering them. But what if it's the other way around?* asks the writer. Can you imagine everything it took, and how long, to come to terms with this question as a given?

I remember the first time I walked into a teacher's lounge as a teacher, in 1986. I told myself, ah, well, here nothing is going to be possible. The size of the room, the style of the furniture, the look of the staff. It wasn't the feeling of something immutable but of something stronger, something more resistant, that wouldn't let you do anything (I remember a biology teacher's green eyes, her intractable flesh). Was it because ten years earlier, they'd seen Nelly burst in, pinning up her MLAC tracts all over the place, her rage, her cheerfulness, and her promise to start all over, from A to Z? Never again! said the teachers! Get her gone already! That she and hers and he and theirs would be gone!

It wouldn't have occurred to me to doubt how the institution changes you, in 1986, at the end of a harsh ten-year war, a lost war, against the family institution. To this day, my poet friends tend to talk more about *playing* with institutions, seeking to divert their routines or latent conventions from the inside, by misdirecting writing practices (evaluations, cover letters, etc.), or *investigating* their function to reveal the salient features—enormities in and of themselves. It's not only the mocking, Swiftian\* use of poetry that I like—and what else is there, when the other side is convinced that more than living life this way of operating is natural, has no alternative?

I can see François, a friend of mine: Sure, but what about Saint-Alban . . .

Saint-Alban is this psychiatric hospital in the Lozère, where, during the war, the second one, Tosquelles, a psychiatrist, worked with caretakers and patients, demolishing the perimeter walls, cooking, gardening, hiding resistance fighters and eating all at a time when thousands of patients in France were starving (Artaud in Rodez, calling for taters). And it was precisely because they were perishing at every asylum in France that the psychiatric institution at Saint-Alban was able to free itself, not because all the taters in all the asylums rained down on the Lozère, but because they were dealing with

---

\* Jonathan Swift published *A Modest Proposal for Preventing the Children of Poor People from Being a Burthen to Their Parents or Country, and for Making Them Beneficial to the Publick* (1729)—a logical proposition: all parents need to do is eat their children.

the mad, the nobodies worth nothing, and good for nothing: they might as well perish; you can do whatever you want with them, as long as you don't try to generalize your little experiment to include the non-mad, who still might be good for something.

And then it was in the Lozère. Have you ever set foot in the Lozère? The department of Lozère, fortunately for it, doesn't exist; it's a bit like D., the town where I live and whose main street Nelly trotted up and down in 1975. Most people put it in the Sud-Ouest or in the Drôme, and I tell them: Yea, that's about right.

The worst that could happen—what I tell myself and tell you right after—is we'll end up in the Lozère, at 900 meters elevation and three hours away from any town; we'll grow taters; we'll divert electricity and give a jar of jam and a carton of eggs to the rural warden so he leaves us the hell alone. This is one type of relation conceivable, in the future, with the institution.

\*

Relatively speaking, Wissembourg, in the mid-'70s, is a bit like the Saint-Alban of the French education system, Marguerite tells me. Wissembourg is way up all the way up at the very top of the north-eastern tip of the Hexagon, on the German border. It's where we put all the problem teachers, pedophiles, and anarchists. So, Nelly, reinstated at the start of the 1976–1977 school year, turns up in Wissembourg, Bas-Rhin, made friends with a history teacher, and organized an exhibition on Wissembourg during the Occupation . . . When Marguerite comes face-to-face with her that year, she sees her in tip-top shape, perhaps invigorated by what just happened to her in D. The girls make use of the opportunity to set up a feminist group, FFF (for Faisant Fonction de Femme, or *Acting as Women*). They are contacted by Xavière Gauthier and put together a special issue of *Sorcières*, her review, which had been in print for two years. When Hans Martin Schleyer, ex-SS officer, jointly responsible for the extermination policy in occupied Czechoslovakia and chairman of the German Employers' Association since the late 1960s, is executed by the Red Army Faction in 1977, they take part in night actions, chanting *We-are-all / German terroristas*, refusing to observe the minute's silence. That's when the trouble started, and Marguerite loses track of Nelly after that—did she go on to work in theater? At the Éducation nationale? I used to take for granted her definitive reinstatement in 1981, under Mitterand. Maybe she never quit as a teacher.

In March 2021, just as I'm hoping to finally wrap up this text, I come across a few lines by her in a report she wrote in 1987 for the Jan Hus Association, an association of intellectuals whose aim was to support Czech teachers and students: "Perestroika, whether innocent or cunning, will melt repression, and the intellectuals will wallow in an element we know well: mud. One takes to hoping that a god will preserve them from the mud carried in by the agonistic flow of commodities."

Françoise told me that in Grenoble, after she herself ran into trouble, she did hard factory work for a while and lived in a community, the Moselle community, on rue de la Moselle, now a little yellow and gray ordinary street, on Street View. The community was all girls, not deliberately but because it was linked to feminism, with the struggle for abortion and contraceptive rights. In another community, she remembers catching lice. But what she remembers best and tells me about in detail, in a letter dated April 23, 2019, is the factory. COTHERM, in La Tronche. BOIS & CHASSANDE, on rue Ampère. MERLIN-GERIN in Meylan. TÉLÉMÉCANIQUE, still in Grenoble. There she worked as a semiskilled laborer, recruited by small temp agencies "that popped up and vanished without notice, making it impossible to get confirmation of employment letters. BOIS & CHASSANDE," she writes, "was a monster-sized factory: from the very moment I set foot in there, I'm in Chaplin's *Modern Times* or Eisenstein's *Strike*. BUT WITH NOISE. The machines are blackened as if from smoke—but there is no smoke, everything is electric. On my way to the automated machines I've been assigned to, there's a HUGE PRESS that looks about 6–8 meters tall. Come to think of it, I wonder if it isn't the machine's giantism that imposed on me the notion of a hellish noise—anyway, now I'm incapable of depicting the noise.

The machine I work on is a drill press. I dip into a huge bag at my feet. I dip in with my hands—unprotected hands—and back out with metal workpieces the size and shape of a wallflower: a cylindrical calyx out of which four petals open up, but the four petals end in a triangle which is at a 90° angle from the petals' plane; these workpieces have been soaked ahead of time in semi-solid, semi-liquid black grease to limit the overheating that will result when, after having loaded the two vertical slides with the pieces picked from the vat, the calice-tube pops up under the two taps—mounted on camshafts—which, perpendicular to the slides, will cut screw threads on the insides of the calice-tubes. More than anything the job results in painful and infected wounds under the fingernails when tapping—which has to be fast—pointy pieces covered in grease barehanded.

The other aspect is that a portion of the salary is output-based. And there's solidarity in fighting output-based labor. One worker, a woman with a Maghrebian background, who can work only at a much higher than average pace—and gets used by management to establish the output on top of which bonuses are then supposed to be paid—hides the surplus parts produced by her labor in the nooks and crannies of the factory so that they won't count toward the base pay in the calculation of bonuses. At the end of a few weeks, I come to understand that the hiring of temp workers is intended to break the resistance of the women workers, who refuse to accept shift work in two periods: 1) so-called 'night-shift' work for the women: 5 a.m.–1 p.m.; 2) 1 p.m.–9 p.m. I 'tendered my resignation' after three or four weeks."

An agrégée teacher working in a factory in the early 1970s, in my book that makes you an établie, a radical who forwent intellectual labor to go into the factory: "Whether and how these hirings relate to the politics of 'établissement' lauded at the time by the Maoist Gauche prolétarienne, there is no relation," Françoise writes and underlines. Establishing oneself presupposes having had the option of giving up a professionally advantageous position to then wind up in the holds of the machine-society. That's not how it went for me since I didn't abandon anything—my situation just wasn't that favorable.

On the phone, Françoise insists on the fact that she is from Pau, and that she never said she *once prepped for the Normale supérieure*: I once prepped for Fontenay. Just as when it was me who took (and failed) the competitive exams, in 1984, there were four normales supérieures: the top (Ulm and Sèvres) and bottom schools (Fontenay and Saint-Cloud), selection within selection. "There were separate recruitments, with a large gap between," Françoise says, who took prep courses, in Paris, for a provincial placement.

I hesitate before I look into Françoise's personal history—a father who was arrested by the Gestapo, a grandfather mailman who didn't pay his taxes and kept in his saddlebag the little blues (telegrams) that notified the farmers of their expropriation: men who were more rebellious than the militant activists, she says—I hesitate before looking for the differences between her and

Nelly, after all the trouble they had in common at the Éducation nationale.

The reason the former took it on the chin, concluding her life as a teacher with: "I didn't love my years teaching middle school, before losing my license and after being reinstated. I avoided the teacher's lounge . . . and aside from several isolated students, I didn't have any relationships I'd be happy to mention."

The reason the latter seemed to sparkle everywhere she went, impressing writers, actors, directors, without every really working in the theater world, having as her best friend, while she was stationed in Bamako, Mamadou Lamine Traoré, the famous underground communist opponent who became Mali's Minister of National Education in 2002—up until his death in 2007, only a few months after Nelly's.

Had the inhabitants of D. sized her up accurately, the Parisian, this snooty and sunny woman, who had come down from the capital to humiliate them a little more, to sleep with their sons and husbands?

\*

<u>The vagina has to have blood; where does one get blood?</u> I made a note and put a box around this sentence of Françoise's. I remember very well that in the moment I wasn't sure exactly what she was talking about, but since the era and its episodes revolved around abortion, it must have had something to do with it.

=> The slaughterhouse. You get blood in the slaughterhouses. The girls from the Moselle commune used to take animal blood from slaughterhouses. Used to simulate miscarriages before going to the ER or the doctor. *At Moselle they knew how to do it* —the catchphrase that used to go around Grenoble. And in D.? They'd give you an abortion in the backroom of a café. If there were any issues, they would call a doctor from Aix. It was organized. No need for a slaughterhouse.

The tears of anguish shed by all these women who knew they were pregnant.


Nelly's enemy number one, in D., was the prosecutor: an antiabortion militant. Without him, there would have been no Cavallero affair in D., nor this book as a result. The most serious offense for the people of D., whether Catholic or worse, Puritans without realizing it, animated by a tacit revulsion for sex: the militants of MLAC, who made others pronounce the forbidden word *abortion*, and by association, *vagina*, *blood*, *embryo*, all of which one wanted to know nothing about, unless through the operation of the Holy Spirit or Nature . . . the worse offense, was it that—or the queers?

Among Rochefort's large volume of novelistic works, *Springtime in the Parking Lot* sits roughly in the middle—1969. The narrator is a runaway teen whose exact age we will never know for certain. One day he left, just like that, as was common in 1969. His father tells him to move! he's blocking the TV, so he leaves. He bumps into some students at a university library, an unusual thing for a guy with a prole background. He wanders around Paris with them, they go to cafés and make vague but cutting cracks at each other. Slowly, bit by bit, and shortly before the end of the book, both we and the narrator come to understand that he has fallen hard in love with Thomas, that they love each other—". . . And because I'm losing myself at each turn I have a head shooting out blossoms in every direction, I don't know what's happening with me"—and that they make love, the student Thomas and him, who must be around fifteen: "I'm so sick of the whole thing about kids. I first made love at thirteen-and-a-half, and even then I was still behind some others," writes Rochefort, perhaps remembering herself at fourteen or fifteen, when it was all about who was going to be the first to *do it*.

Several weeks ago, as I was reading *Springtime in the Parking Lot*, I went for a look around on the social network Copains d'avant, in search of a girl I knew in elementary school, and lost track of in middle school, then ran into on the street not far from my place, with some dudes who looked older to me but must have been around sixteen. It was her who made me touch the little budding mound of her breasts, in fifth grade, while we showered after the swimming pool, and who laughed as she told me, two years later, that she had hidden her boyfriend in her bed when her mother came knocking at her door, in the morning. I have no idea how many girls had already made love in middle school, in the late 1970s—probably the same amount as in 1950 or 1960—with the added fear of getting pregnant (this girlfriend had gone on the pill early).

There are these words from the narrator, and from Christiane Rochefort, very similar to Faraldo's film released two years later: "... just like that, with no drama, in simple joy, the heroes not at all guilty, indeed delighted, in good spirits, fulfilled, at least temporarily, and covered in feathers ..." (they had just had a pillow fight). And, for at least three years, from 1969 to 1971, a small part of the French population was able to subscribe to this sentence, formulate similar ones, live in agreement, while thinking that the infinite prospect opening up before them was that of another world, radiantly so. The more one made revolution, the more one made love.

The more one made love, the more one made revolution.

Then the two disengaged from each other. In surrender. Then the second was forgotten.

Once, in the heat of June 2020, Joseph would go on to spell it out: *flesh and verb were inseparable*. At the time, his meaning mostly eluded me—these aren't the words I would use ... I would say (the epoch would say): sex. Joseph often recounts this unforgettable memory, how they were making love, and while still in bed, after, the girl had talked to him about Bataille\* ... How there was continuity in erotism but discontinuity in life ... How they spoke on and on ...

Sex and *parole*? language? In any case, we don't

---

\* Georges Bataille (1897–1962), *L'Érotisme* (Minuit, 1957), published in English as *Erotism: Death & Sensuality* (City Lights Books, 1962).

associate the two; sex has gone silent. We don't see why it leads to this or that political (or philosophical) discussion is apparent either. That sex no longer speaks implies therefore a language without flesh—the vacant language of corporate French, the ordinary French one speaks every day, which drips from our mouths like pearls of the gutter without one's being able to retain a single one. Just as the epoch speaks through us in order to exist and chases us away from our past, from our memory, kept away from it with a sudden sweeping hand gesture, with a hands off, those who lived through those years, if they want to explain themselves, if they want to check in our eyes to see whether we are capable of grasping at a distance the fusion of flesh and words which we were unable to experience, having been born too late (sometimes only five, eight years too late), they must slowly by successive evolutions, make this past arise in them, the way one shakes a blanket over a fire to make smoke signals.

And so, sex remained alone—lashed to the principles of love, of procreation, or to liberal and neoliberal mechanisms, which Jarry anticipated in *The Supermale* (the politician screwing in time-lapse at the Sofitel between two air conditioners; the industrial and cokehead phase of porn). But,

That sex is politics, fags, dykes, this they knew a thing or two about at the very least. They still know—as this book tries to put the past in the present, and even more importantly, when it comes to literature, the present in the present.

# 7

In autumn 2019, I asked N.G. to come over and tell me about the time she was hitchhiking regularly—I wanted to draw comparisons with what Gilberte told me about Nelly, that she used to love truck drivers (I cite) and solo hitchhiking, that this was how she traveled through Eastern Europe and that her main game, as it were, was to make love with her truck drivers at the end of the trip.

The period during which N.G. hitchhiked frequently, when she was between seventeen and twenty-five, was the '90s. Her thing was to talk a lot, because if you let the silence set in for too long, it creates an embarrassing situation—like in other situations, N.G. adds in an email: "Think about it, you're in your kitchen with a guy who's not saying anything, whom you don't know at all, so you've got no idea where his thoughts are headed . . . The truck drivers' solitude only intensifies that dynamic, how their cab is a universe to itself where they actually live (not far from their bed, etc.). One time, I couldn't get a guy to talk, then at some point he shows me his gun, all without saying anything!"

So she would talk to them a lot and they gradually would open up and tell her about their lives. Invariably it would start with: See, I'm fine, but there's some other drivers I know . . . Eventually they let loose: five-day routes that actually take a whole week, Saturdays for sleeping and Sundays for getting back on the road; three weeks on the job and a week to rest which is whittled down to four days; you don't see your kids anymore, you don't see your wife; the separations, the divorces, the challenges of having a girlfriend ("I can't get a girlfriend)—"Three times, they cried in front of me." She remembers them as men who were quite touching, happy to be able to confide in someone, rarely demanding.

N.G. shares her most recent hitchhiking anecdotes with me. Last summer, for example, between the Larzac and the Mediterranean, south of Montpellier, a guy driving to go kitesurfing, then a guy in a Jaguar, then a young chick who drove a truck who was a frequent hitchhiker like herself, and then a guy from a military base, and it goes on like that! Or even the guy who said to her, "People like you I usually hear only on the radio," and then drove her over 100 kilometers.

Well then, superimposed on Nelly's image, both rebellious and radiant girl, certified agrégée Parisian, was that of the desirous hitchhiker, a figure out of the 1970s, when hitchhiking was only a means of moving from one place to another while poor or because there were no trains, no buses where you lived.

\*

The end justifies the means, Nelly thought, Marguerite tells me. That's how power speaks—not my way of speaking. But if they made it theirs, in the early '70s, before the great discouragement, maybe it's because they understood that only a counterpower with a force of wording equal to that of power would be capable of beating it, or at least weakening it. Indeed, it was symbolically weakened by actions; made weak by all those girls who fucked politically (as in, not just anyhow and not with just anyone, even if that is how some imagined it), those crowds of workers having come for their due, those students in the factories, those intellectuals clearly (physically) showing what side they were on . . . And I really do like the phrase, the end justifies the means, but as situated, within the scope of tactics, not in general.

At the end of the day, even if, Marguerite tells me, Nelly never gained institutional recognition—for the institution to recognize someone like her was impossible—that woman was a teacher extraordinaire. Which ones—men, women, children—gain institutional recognition, by the way? Hard workers and wily foxes. The institution churns out its fair share of hard workers and wily foxes who are innocent at times, capable of regurgitating *appropriate* and coded speech about work-in-progress which, from across the table, always illuminates you, like the moon. It's not at all unlikely that in passing Nelly would have put one of these inspectors in his place (along with multiple heads of school, scores of colleagues, and students—can you see her *holding her tongue*?).

Finally, she was a teacher right up until the end, before undertaking studies of history in retirement, always with a fervor (a flame) which arose not so much from some hidden point in her being, as from her past as a proletarian daughter. From her father, Italian émigré and mason, Marguerite clarifies. From her mother, shoe saleswoman (thank you very much). From her birth in the city of Toulon, which she hated.

And was Nelly always elegant and well-dressed? Marguerite (or Gilberte) laughs: she didn't give a shit. The black cape caused a sensation over nothing no doubt, just like the djellaba that belonged to X., the gay farmer's son; redneck's son, queer and visibly proud of it, or at least someone whose being proud of it didn't make for too many problems, in those years.

I ask Marguerite what Nelly read, and whether she wrote. She replies that she struggled with literature, read no novels, some poetry, all that was too conventional for her though; she liked to read Lyotard, and then Plato.

Just as Patrick persists in posing the question of chaos, and whether it is livable, Nelly always posed the question of the rule and its transgression.

*

Nearly at the end now, and I have no more ideas for anything else to add to this text when I meet Hélène, in Manosque, at a café, on this day, June 10, 2020. She pulls out *Moby Dick* and sets it on the table: "So we recognize one another, I'll be holding *Moby Dick*!"—and, in another text message: "I'm still in favor of us seeing each other and talking, especially since there are inaccuracies and fantasies in what you were told about Nelly."

It's too bad, she starts off, only two or three years ago, I could still remember it all . . . But now, it's so long ago . . . You know, Gabrielle Russier*. . . Back then, there was a colleague who supported her, along with others . . . Gabrielle's son found her, some years ago. He wanted her to talk to him about his mother . . . but she had lost her memory . . .

These will likely be the last years to hear from these witnesses, squashed between the celebration of the veterans and blowhards of their time. A generation I picture as basking in the sun without fear for several months, when I was a kid.

Hélène corrects: at one time, Nelly had participated in a cooperative, in Algeria; she had wanted to stay. But the person who went on to become one of the directors of the Islamic Salvation Front, Abbassi Madani, told her:

---

* In 1967, lit teacher Gabrielle Russier had an affair with one of her students, the sixteen-year-old Christian Rossi. Sentenced to a one-year suspended prison sentence, she ended her life in 1969. Christian Rossi, in 1971: "It was not at all a passion. It was love. Passion is not lucid. Now in this case, it was lucid. [. . .] The [two years] of memories she left me, she left them all to me, I don't have to talk about them. I feel them. I lived them, I alone. [. . .] As for the rest, people know the story: a woman whose name was Gabrielle Russier. We loved each other, she was thrown in prison, she killed herself. It's simple."

"But you were never a teacher here, Madame . . . ," and so she left. Back from Algeria, she invested in a restaurant, in the Cevennes, with a girl she trusted blindly who then went dark in nothing flat.

And then there was the sex, says Hélène, which did interest her, but not as much as intelligence . . . She was an intellectual, after all . . . When she spotted an intelligent man, she wouldn't let up . . . but she wasn't particularly eager to fuck, Hélène made plain to me, and anyway, "big dick" isn't something she would have said . . . That wasn't how she talked . . . She was very direct with men but paradoxically, she was very modest in the way she talked about them. She certainly did enjoy being provocative . . . So she may have said it like that . . . as a provocation . . .

And then her father wasn't a bricklayer, not at all . . . He was an engineer at the Toulon naval port . . . And her mother was a saleswoman in a luxury menswear store . . .

What is certain, Hélène continues, is that she should have never been a high school teacher, she should have been teaching college . . . Every time she was burning it down . . . The principal of a school in the Var requested her transfer . . . He had all the parents behind him. One time, they switched her class with one of her friend's classes . . . And then this friend's students, they all ended up crying . . .

She recalls how fifteen years before the case, *Le Monde* had titled "D., a town where nothing ever happens" . . . And then it was the scandal pages that drew her attention, and she came up from Marseille, with friends, to support Nelly—within a hair's breadth of being accused of pimping . . . and hence prison . . . This is how they met.

If there's one thing to understand about the whole story, adds Hélène, the whole story of what happened to her in D., it's that she never recovered from it.

Several months ago, there were maybe thirty of us at the office of a local assemblywoman, a fickle social democrat with no distinguishing features—a politician. We'd demanded a meeting about the pension reforms, what she did or did not vote for, what her position was. This assemblywoman then tried hard to pick apart bit by bit what would be most convenient in general when responding to the precise questions put to her, alternately going under and resurfacing, malignant and lost, intelligent and self-assured. The same type of staff, in D., must have decided to cleanse the city of this irritating teacher who intended to speak the truth, relieved by how its restless youth would end up going silent, leaving, or dying for a fix.

In an earlier version, I made a note that Nelly wanted to be buried with a funeral mass—she did not have the faith, but perhaps this was the last opportunity for a logical wager for her, in the Pascalian spirit. Hélène corrects: after a short stay in a deplorable Establishment of Accommodation for Dependent Old Persons, she entrusted her mother to a Catholic institution and encountered a remarkable priest there, a philosopher-priest. Before dying, he asked her to edit a text, and this text was read at her funeral by the man to whom she was married for more than thirty-five years.

*

The following story begins in a church. Mass commences, in distant times—let's just say the church is full. The scene is set in the countryside right next to a forest. Gunshots ring out. A man perks up his ears. Three boys come running into the nave out of breath and worked up, we flushed out a stag! The man immediately rises, climbs over the pew, dashes toward the door and mounts his horse that has been waiting for him there, held by the bridle by another boy. The hunt is on. They track the stag, who runs zigzags, whom they glimpse in flashes, from inside tree trunks they pull out bark chips masquerading as deer fur, and they ride at full gallop for hours, in pursuit of the stag, which eludes them at lightning speed, the horses' hind-hooves sinking into the soft humus, rumps in the air, on the horses' necks they ride and they ride. Then, the wind, it also rises. It is terrible. It hoots and howls from some black speck in the forest, shaking the leaves for several seconds before blowing them off and raising them in bundles, flung at the hunters' heads, caught in a hailstorm that wounds their faces and hands. The strength of the storm gradually raises the whole horde itself off the ground: the wind pushes under the panicked horses' bellies, who are shifting from right to left, being tripped up in the trees, brushing against the canopies, under the bulging eyes of the cavaliers who stretch their torsos toward a land beyond reach. But the hunter still wants his part of the game, of the stag he sees dead: *Go and hunt!* He bays into the whirlwind. Then, corpses fall around him and on his horse, intact or in pieces.

I no longer remember exactly when Patrick evoked this legend, most likely on a farmer's market day standing on the boulevard, as he spoke about sound, trying to explain to me the difference between verticality of sound, which lasted until the seventeenth century, and the transition to horizontality—peasants in the factories, in the plants, the sirens, the bombshells, the disabling sounds used in the Palestinian territories and at demonstrations.

This book, borne of Patrick's insistence (you can though, you can do it), of a prosecutor's dirty tricks and of the politics and determination of a woman, I wrote in large part during the strikes of 2019—I don't know if I'll still be able to write books in this form in a month or a year, just as nobody in the present day knows whether they'll still be able to live in the same way ("as before") in a month or in a year.

On the last page of *History Against Tradition*,* Augustín García Calvo writes he did "nothing more than reference what had been, what had taken place, in formulae that were the most purely predicative and descriptive; but for *Tradition Against History* I ought to move on from phrases to different modalities, to exhortative and votive phrases, like 'Do not continue!,' 'Do otherwise whoever can!' [...] and others in the same style."

It's hard not to think of the 1973 film, *Order*,** and its final warning: "Stop while there's still time, stop."

---

* Augustín García Calvo, *Histoire contre tradition* (Éditions la Tempête, 2019).
** A film by Jean-Daniel Pollet.

## AUTHOR'S NOTE

I thank warmly and most especially:

Patrick, Vincent, Béa, Françoise (from Grenoble), Françoise (from Mézel), Marguerite, Hélène and Gilberte, as well as Cathy, Dany, N.G., Leslie, Stephen, Stéphane, François, Joseph, Philippe, Marc, and Isabelle.

Citations on pages 84 to 86 are drawn from *Avec des cœurs acharnés* (*Tenacious hearts*; Claude Courchay, Gallimard, 1978).

Citation from an extract of Nelly Cavallero's report for the Jan Hus Association: https://www.cairn.info/revue-bulletin-de-l-institut-pierre-renouvin-2020-1-page-71.htm#no26

## TRANSLATOR'S NOTE

When I first emailed Nathalie Quintane about *La Cavalière* in April 2024, I included one trailing-off question about the use of tense in the book (the lack of the imperfect in English remains vexing). She replied quickly and generously to my questions, but added that the decision-making in her writing is generally more aleatory; in terms of the tenses, nothing specific or intentionally circumspect was at stake. My aim has been to transfer the dense knit of simultaneous timelines in substance and feeling with sensitivity to the aleatory impulses that produced the original as much as possible. It's my hope that this translation might contribute some small part to Quintane's *mise à jour* by which the wayward urgencies and lessons of the post-'68 years might be updated to gain us a better hold in the here and now.

I have tried to briefly contextualize historical or cultural terms in text whenever possible. The footnotes are the author's; for readers interested in a little more background on phrases or terms and their contexts, see the notes that follow.

\*

Page 9
**150 francs**— About $210 USD in 2024.

Page 21
**Yellow Vests** (*Les Gilets jaunes*)—Yellow Vest Movement. The national riots unleashed one year into French President Emmanuel Macron's first term after he proposed a raise on the fuel tax (excluding jet and freighter fuel), purportedly to mitigate climate change. The tax would have especially impacted rural populations with long commutes, already suffering from rising costs of living and cuts to rail service. On November 17, 2018, 300,000 protesters blockaded traffic in yellow safety vests (which all French motorists are required to keep in their vehicles). By December, the clashes between the *Gilets jaunes* and the police in the streets of Paris grew increasingly violent, with the CRS, France's anti-riot police, making full use of newly acquired so-called non-lethal armaments. By the summer of 2019, 1,797 police and gendarmes and 2,448 protestors had been injured.

Page 23, 26, 52, 55, 65, 72–73, 82, 89, 93
**Éducation nationale**—French ministry for education. France's largest employment domain and its largest single budgetary item. All educators in France are considered civil servants, and the right to education is stipulated by the French constitution.

Page 24, 92, 100
**Agrégé·e·s**—Agrégation is the extremely rigorous and prestigious exam for lycée (high school equivalent) teachers. *Agrégé·e·s* teachers have more protections, placement options, lighter teaching loads, and more research or lecturing responsibilities. The other competitive exam for French teachers confers the title *professeu·r·e·s certifié·e·s*, which also affords teachers certain protections and benefits, and includes both *collège* (roughly middle school) and *lycée* teachers.

Pages 25, 33–35
***Midi Libre, Nice-Matin, Ici Paris, France Soir, France Dimanche, Le Monde, Nouvel Obs***—*Midi Libre* is a regional daily newspaper based in southern France; *Nice-Matin* is a regional daily newspaper covering Nice and the Provence-Alpes-Côtes d'Azur region of southeastern France; *Ici Paris* is a national weekly celebrity magazine; *France Soir* is a non-specialized daily newspaper; *France Dimanche* is a weekly celebrity magazine; *Le Monde* is a daily afternoon newspaper and one of France's newspapers of record; *Le Nouvel Obs* is a prominent weekly news magazine.

Page 33, 47
**Rencontres Cinéma**—A film festival format popular in France, particularly in smaller towns and mid-sized cities.

Pages 36, 55, 66, 68
**Maspero; *Repression in Education***—François Maspero (1932–2015) was a central figure of the far left in the '60s, '70s, and '80s. A bookseller, author, translator, and journalist,

he's mostly known for his eponymous publishing venture that he founded in 1959 at the height of the Algerian War. Authors such as Frantz Fanon, Louis Althusser, Võ Nguyên Giáp, and other revolutionaries were first published in French by Maspero. In 1972, the review *L'École émancipée* published *La Répression dans l'enseignment* under the Maspero imprint, which took an inventory of the repressive measures levied by the Éducation nationale against teachers seeking to implement reforms after the events of '68.

Page 40, 60
**les banlieues, banlieusarde**—suburbs, suburbanite. The French word for "suburb" is *banlieue*, though the latter tends to be demographically distinct from its U.S. counterpart in terms of its peripheral situation relative to the more wealthy urban center. In the U.S., on the other hand, suburbs were primarily developed in the 1960s onward with the aim of walling suburbanites off from the underfunded cities (e.g., through "white flight"). For more background on Saint-Denis, see Benoît Bréville's "Why Parisians fear and loathe Saint-Denis" from the August 2022 English edition of *Le Monde Diplomatique*.

Page 49
**journey up to Paris** (*la montée à Paris*)—A literary phrase invoking the archetypal (primarily in nineteenth-century literature) journey in which a young man sets out from the provinces for the metropole in an attempt to improve his station in life, usually an ultimately doomed venture; Balzac's *Lost Illusions* would be one classic of the genre.

## Page 52
**PTT** (*Postes, Télégraphes et Téléphones*)—Postal services, Telegraphs, and Telephones. The former French administration of postal services and telecommunications. In the fall of 1974, the workers at PTT participated in what is now known as the "big strike," which also involved bank and railway workers.

## Pages 52, 86, 94
**MLAC** (*Mouvement pour la liberté de l'avortement et de la contraception*)—Movement for free abortion and contraception. A group that agitated for voluntary termination of pregnancy provided on request and paid for by social security as a medical procedure. The movement dissolved in 1975 after the Veil Act decriminalizing abortion passed.

**explication de texte**—explanation of text. A French formalist method of literary study and pedagogical tool, particularly in philosophy courses, to develop students' ability to close read literary texts.

## Page 59, 62
**Bac diploma** (*bac, baccalauréat*)—The *bac* is the final examination covering a broad range of subjects that students must pass to complete their final year (*la terminale*) of secondary schooling.

## Page 61
**Académie française**—The French Academy. The principal French council on matters of language, established in 1635 by Cardinal Richelieu, who served as the chief minister to King

Louis XIII. Writers of repute such as historian and journalist **Pierre Gaxotte** (1895–1982) frequently sit on the academy.

**Reduced hours**—*Le chantage à l'emploi* (literally "employment blackmail") covers a variety of methods and strategies used by employers to force workers to accept lower wages, fewer hours, and other unfavorable work conditions. These may take the form of transfers, relocations, worksite closures, relinquishing of benefits, tighter monitoring and surveillance of workers, or more oblique methods like threatening regulators that they would sooner terminate their employees than negotiate.

## Page 63

**zones to defend** (*zone à defendre; ZAD*)—In northern France, near Nantes, in 2009, a 4,000-acre area of wetlands, fields, and forests was declared a *zone d'aménagement différé*, i.e., a *zad*, or a "deferred development area" to prepare the way for an international airport. But farmers refused to sell their land to the government, and activists and locals occupied the land and renamed it a *ZAD*, a *zone-à-defendre*, a zone to defend. After a protracted struggle both on the ground and in court, the airport was finally canceled in 2018 (See: Mauvaise Troupe Collective (tr. Kristin Ross), *The Zad and NoTAV: Territorial Struggles and the Making of a New Political Intelligence* (Verso, 2017).

## Page 65, 72

**A4/A5**—A4 paper is sized at 8.27 x 11.69 inches and A5 paper at 5.82 × 8.26 inches. They function as letter and memo paper, respectively.

Page 78
**WLM** (*Mouvement de libération des femmes*)—MLF, or Women's Liberation Movement. The feminist movement founded in 1970 in France to militate for the bodily autonomy of women.

Page 81, 92
**École(s) normale(s) supérieure(s)**—Specialized top-level universities. Originally founded in 1794 during the French revolution, these are elite academic institutions with extremely rigorous and competitive admissions processes.

Page 95
**Copains d'avant**—Literally, "friends from before." A French social network founded in 2001, intended for people to reconnect with old classmates and colleagues.

Page 92
**Établie**—In the 1970s, members of the Maoist group GP (Gauche-prolétarienne) left behind nascent intellectual careers and entered factories as laborers. The French term for these workers, établi·e·s, references both the establishment (*l'établissement*) to which they had belonged and their new stations, the proverbial workbenches known as *établis*. An analogous strategy of seeking employment at a non-unionized workplace with the goal of unionizing it is known as *salting* in the U.S.; where salts' primary objective is to unionize a workplace, the établi·e·s committed to the Maoist practice of the *enquête*, the investigation into proletarian consciousness by "going to the people" and inquiring about their local situations

on the ground and relying on these findings to direct their organizing strategy. For a first-hand account of the GP organizing efforts, see Robert Linhart's *L'établi* (*The Assembly Line*, tr. Margaret Crosland), originally published in 1978.

### Page 108
**Augustin García Calvo**—Spanish philologist, philosopher, poet, and playwright (1926–2012) who was exiled from Spain during the Franco dictatorship. For an overview on Calvo as a thinker, see Vicente Ordóñez's article "Augustin García Calvo in our time" in *Radical Philosophy*, issue 2.03, December 2018.

## ACKNOWLEDGMENTS

The Hölderlin phrase in the footnote on page 65 is Michael Hamburger's translation. My translation of the Blanchot quotation in the footnote on page 16 draws on Charlotte Mandell's translation.

I wish to thank Nathalie, Stephen, and Patrick for welcoming me to Digne in April 2024 and for the many conversations around the book. Thanks also to CITL for hosting me in Arles to work on this translation.

Thank you to David L. Ulin of *Air/Light* for publishing an excerpt of *The Cavalier* as well as David Buuck for publishing an account of my trip to Digne in Tripwire 21.

Thank you to Matvei Yankelevich for taking on this project and making it into a book and also to Catherine Taylor for the elucidating comments on the manuscript.

And thank you as ever to Wendy, for turning these sentences over and over with me.

**NATHALIE QUINTANE** is a French poet and writer living in Digne-les-Bains, France. She has published more than 25 books in essentially every genre, most of which have appeared with the publishing houses P.O.L. and La Fabrique. Quintane's writing distinguishes itself by the recombination of memoir, prose poem, narration, reportage, tract, journalism, autofiction, pastiche, literary criticism, etc. into new literary forms. In the 1990s, Quintane began publishing and performing in Marseille alongside poets Christophe Tarkos and Stéphane Bérard, with whom she established the poetry review RR, which parodied the literary establishment. Beginning with her first books, *Chaussure* (Shoe) and *Remarques* (Remarks), her writing has continued resisting the fixed style of *la belle langue* (beautiful language) that dominates the global literary marketplace, while also seeking to destabilize the over-reliance on derivative stylings among the insurrectionary left. Two of her books, *Joan Darc* and *Tomatoes*, have previously appeared in English translation with La Presse and Kenning Editions, respectively. Quintane was the last recipient of the Prix du Zorba (otherwise known as the Anti-Goncourt award) in 2018 for her book *Un oeil en moins* (One Eye Less).

**JONATHAN LARSON** is a translator-poet living in Brooklyn. His translation of Francis Ponge's *Nioque of the Early-Spring* and Friederike Mayröcker's *Scardanelli* were both published by The Song Cave and his translation of Mayröcker's *From Embracing the Sparrow-wall, or 1 Schumann-madness* was published by OOMPH! Press. He is currently working on his own book project titled *Idiomatic*.

*The Cavalier* by Nathalie Quintane
Copyright © P.O.L, 2021
Translation copyright © Jonathan Larson, 2025

Originally published in French as *La Cavalière* by P.O.L éditeur (Paris, 2021).

ISBN 978-1-959708-15-5
LCCN 2025944592

First Edition, 2025 — 2,500 copies

Winter Editions, Brooklyn, New York
wintereditions.net

Distributed by Asterism (US) and Public Knowledge (UK)

The cover image is a detail of an article from *Le Monde*, May 31, 1976, related to the case of Nelly Cavallero.

Cet ouvrage a bénéficié du Programme d'aide à la publication de l'Institut français. (This book has been published with the support of the Programme d'aide à la publication of the Institut français.)

WE is grateful for the support of our subscribers, and extends special thanks to recent Supporting and Lifetime Subscribers: Anonymous [2], Anonymous (in memory of the Beaubiens), Yevgeniy Fiks, Katy Lederer.

WE books are typeset in Heldane, a renaissance-inspired serif designed by Kris Sowersby for Klim Type Foundry, and Zirkon, a contemporary gothic designed by Tobias Rechsteiner for Grilli Type. This book was printed and bound in Lithuania by BALTO print with Munken papers. Manufactured by Arctic Paper in Sweden, Munken meets EU Ecolabel, Forest Stewardship Council, and Cradle to Cradle certification standards.

 Winter Editions

Emily Simon, IN MANY WAYS

Garth Graeper, THE SKY BROKE MORE

Robert Desnos, NIGHT OF LOVELESS NIGHTS, tr. Lewis Warsh

Richard Hell, WHAT JUST HAPPENED

Marina Tëmkina & Michel Gérard, BOYS FIGHT

Claire DeVoogd, VIA

Monica McClure, THE GONE THING

Ahmad Almallah, BORDER WISDOM

Hélio Oiticica, SECRET POETICS, tr. Rebecca Kosick

Heimrad Bäcker, DOCUMENTARY POETRY, tr. Patrick Greaney

Robert Fitterman, CREVE COEUR

Karla Kelsey, TRANSCENDENTAL FACTORY: FOR MINA LOY

Alan Gilbert, THE EVERYDAY LIFE OF DESIGN

Betsy Fagin, FIRES SEEN FROM SPACE

Cristina Pérez Díaz, FROM THE FOUNDING OF THE COUNTRY

Sarah Riggs, LINES

Leah Flax Barber, THE MIRROR OF SIMPLE SOULS

Monique Wittig, THE LESBIAN BODY, tr. David Le Vay

Monique Wittig, ACROSS THE ACHERON, tr. David Le Vay with Margaret Crosland

Nathalie Quintane, THE CAVALIER, tr. Jonathan Larson

Michael Kasper, START ANYWHERE

POSTCARDS OF THE SIEGE: VISUAL CULTURE DURING THE SIEGE OF LENINGRAD (1941–1944), ed. Polina Barskova

Serena Solin, A BARER SKY

James Loop, METRONOME

Jacqueline Waters, THE FRY